A Secret Well Kept

Based on a true story.

This book is a work of fiction.
This book may not be reproduced without written consent from the author.

Special thanks to everyone who
encouraged me to write this book.
Thank you for believing in me!

To my amazing children who inspire me,
and to my wonderful husband who
has supported me in everything,
I Love You!

Although this book is a work of fiction, abuse is not.
It happens to more people than you would believe.
The physical pains of abuse may be temporary, but
the emotional pain isn't.
It affects every relationship you will ever have.
It makes it hard to believe and trust that you won't
get hurt by every person you meet.
It makes every day a struggle not to give in to the
anger and pain that was caused.
Abuse is a lifetime of a completely exhausting game
of "What if...?"
What if I had fought back?
What if the next person I trust does the same thing?
What if...?

It is a mental tug of war between hope and doubt.
It doesn't end.
If you or someone you know has been abused
(physically, mentally, sexually, emotionally, etc.)
please find help. Talk to someone about it.
It is a secret that should *not* be well kept.

Too often abuse goes unnoticed and untold.
Don't be afraid to
Speak Up and Speak Out.

Titanium Heart

Titanium
Unbreakable
Impenetrable
Some people say that they have a wall around their
heart
But I say that there is no wall around my heart
For a wall can be scaled
It can be knocked down
It can be destroyed
No, there is no wall
Instead, my heart is trapped inside a titanium ball
No ending, no beginning
No way for someone to get in
No way for it to be broken
I keep my heart protected inside my ball

I don't worry that my heart will be trampled on
That it will be abused and misused
Nobody can get inside my titanium heart
But neither can I get out
I am trapped in here with all the pain of the past
With everything that happened to my heart before I
forged this ball of protection
I cannot outrun my hurt
I cannot escape my shame
Nobody can hurt me
Nobody can help me

~Anna Wright

The Great Pretender

How long must I pretend?

Pretend that I'm not afraid that everyone will leave me
and I'll be alone?
Just like my dad did.

Pretend that every time a guy talks to me, I'm not
trying to see his hidden motives?
Like when my babysitters "only wanted to play a
game" with me.

Pretend that I'm not ashamed by the things I had to do
as a child?
No matter that he was not.

Pretend that I have fully overcome the pain of trusting
a man who was supposed to protect me?

Pretend that I don't get sick to my stomach every time
I remember?

Pretend that I'm not still angry at those who took
advantage of me when I couldn't protect myself?

Pretend that the past does not still influence my
present relationships?

Pretend to always be strong and not need anyone
when the truth is the complete opposite?

Pretend to be brave while I hide all of my insecurities?

Pretend that, on the inside, I'm not that same little
child that was curled up tight in a ball crying because
the men she believed would protect her stole her
innocence instead?

What would my life be like if I didn't have to put on
this mask every day of my life?

If I didn't have to live every day as the great
pretender?

~Anna Wright

Chapter 1

Confused. That would be the best way to describe how six-year-old, Anna Wright, felt as she lay on the bottom bunk of the bed she shared with her older sister. As she squeezed her doll closer to her chest, she tried not to cry while memories of the day flooded her mind. Nothing seemed right anymore.

"I don't know what to do, Emmie," Anna whispered into the ear of her Cabbage Patch doll. "Everybody really likes Joey, but he did something very bad and now I'm kinda scared."

Emmie was Anna's most trusted friend in the world. She was missing one eye, her clothes and body were stained with everything from dirt to ketchup, and her hair looked like someone had taken a dull pair of scissors to it, but Anna loved Emmie completely. She knew that she could tell Emmie her deepest, most scariest secrets and Emmie would never, ever tell anyone. That was just the kind of friend Emmie was.

Anna froze when she heard her sister moving around on the top bunk. She held her breath, waiting to see if Liza had heard what she was telling Emmie. She would ask too many questions that Anna did not want to answer.

Besides, Liza would probably tell her mommy that she was making up stories again. Anna couldn't help it if no one believed her when she told them she didn't know how the mud got all over the kitchen. How would she know? She didn't even like mud pies. And she didn't know how she got mud in her hair. It must have been when she was laying on the grass watching the clouds pass by...yesterday.

Even at her age, Anna was a very bright little girl and could come up with the craziest of stories without trying. Her mom would normally just shake her head and tell Anna that she was silly.

Anna slowly released her breath when she realized that Liza wasn't awake. Rather than risk anyone hearing what else she was going to tell Emmie, she just kissed her cheek and whispered, "Good night, Emmie. I love you."

But Anna didn't go to sleep. Instead, she lay on her side, curled up into a tight ball, and thought about how a day could go from being the happiest, most wonderful day ever, into the worst nightmare kind of a day in a matter of minutes.

Anna had woken up that morning more excited than when she lost her first tooth. Liza was going to teach her how to skate. In Anna's mind, Liza was the best skater there ever was. Anna jumped out of bed and ran straight to the bathroom. After she and Emmie went potty, she quickly brushed both of their teeth. She knew that her mommy would check them when she got downstairs, so she made sure to brush them extra good.

When she got back to her room, Anna took off her favorite faded Care Bear night gown and quickly put on a pair of green shorts and a purple short sleeve shirt. These were Anna's favorite colors, and she just knew that they would give her luck when she was learning to skate. After slipping on her favorite bright pink socks and her new yellow sneakers, she all but flew down the steps and to the kitchen for breakfast.

"Anna Michelle. How many times have I told you not to run down the stairs?" Melissa asked giving Anna "the look." The one that said, "Do *not* make me tell you again."

"But mommy, there was a giant mouse chasing me! It had super big teeth! And I just knew that if I didn't run, it was going to eat my whole leg off!" Anna exclaimed as she sat down at the table, putting Emmie in the chair next to her.

Melissa chuckled as she turned back to washing the dishes. "Where did you get that from?"

Anna's hand stopped midway between the stack of pancakes in the middle of the table and plopping a second one onto her Dora the Explorer plate. "I got it from the plate, mommy." Sometimes her mommy asked the funniest questions.

Melissa whirled around with a quizzical look on her face. "The plate?"

Anna stared at her mommy for a long moment. "Yes, mommy. Don't you 'member? You put the pancakes on the plate in the middle of the table. That's where I got my pancakes from."

Melissa walked over, placed her hands on the sides of Anna's head and gave her a noisy kiss on the forehead. "You, my dear, are a very clever girl."

Anna beamed up at her. She loved it when her mommy gave her special names like clever. "And Emmie too. She is clever too, right?"

Melissa picked up the old, worn doll while smiling back at Anna. "Absolutely! Emmie too!" She gave the doll's head an even louder kiss, placed her back in the chair and went back to cleaning the dishes.

"Do you know what clever is, Emmie?" She heard Anna whisper. "It means extra special! That's what mommy told me. Me and you are very extra special!"

Melissa smiled to herself. She loved listening to her youngest child's silly bantering with the eight-year-old doll. She remembered how Liza's eyes had lit up the Christmas she found Emmie under the tree. Now, though, Liza said she was way too old to play with baby dolls.

Melissa sighed. Her girls were growing up so fast. It seemed like just yesterday she was bringing Liza home from the hospital, alone and unsure how she was going to raise a baby all by herself. She was happy when her aunt offered to help her, but she couldn't have stayed indefinitely. Then she met George and fell in love. They were married the following year, and the year after that Anna was born. How she wished she could slow time down.

George, on the other hand, could not wait until the girls were older. He hated how she and Liza "coddled to Anna's every whim." Just two days ago he had said, "You have to stop babying her, Melissa. She is almost seven years old, not an infant. It's time for her to start growing up." He had said it so many times that Melissa was sick of hearing it. It seemed they were having the same argument almost every night. She didn't care though. She loved her girls more than life itself and wanted them to have the best childhood she could offer them. If that meant pretending that Emmie was alive, then so be it. It was well worth it when she looked into Anna's big, bright eyes and saw the joy shining through. She would let her kids stay kids for as long as she could, no matter what happened to her.

Anna scraped her chair back from the table, grabbed Emmie, then ran over and gave Melissa a tight hug. "Wish me luck, mommy. Me and Emmie are learning how to skate today!"

Melissa turned and looked down at Anna. "Good luck to you, my angel." She tapped Anna lightly on the nose with her index finger. "And good luck to you, Ms. Emmie," she said plucking the doll on her nose. Squatting down so that she was eye level, she said, "Now you girls be sure to put on your knee and elbow pads and your helmets. Skating can be dangerous, and I don't want my girls getting hurt."

"We will, mommy," Anna said turning away from Melissa and skipping out the back door. "Come on, Emmie, let's go find Liza." Still squatting, Melissa smiled to herself as she watched Anna enthusiastically having a conversation with her doll, when a movement from the doorway caught her attention. She looked over to see George standing in the doorway with an accusatory glare.

"Good morning, George. Would you like some coffee?" Melissa asked standing up quickly, a smile pasted on her face.

Instead of answering, he just walked away.

Turning back to the sink, Melissa's shoulders slumped. She knew there would be a big argument when he got home that night. She could still feel the bruise on her side from the last argument.

Chapter 2

Once on the back deck, Anna stopped and looked around. She had done that for as long as she could remember. She would just stop and look at all the fresh green grass, the new leaves on the trees, the new flowers that were blooming. Then she would close her eyes and listen to all the new baby birds crying for their mommies. Last, she would take in one very slow, deep breath, inhaling the freshness in the air. She loved the spring. Every year her mommy would bring her and Liza out there to see the new flowers that had grown.

"Mommy, why do the flowers have to go away when it's snowy out?" Anna had once asked.

"Because, my darling, just like you sleep at night to rest, the earth sleeps in the wintertime. God made it like that so things could grow bigger and stronger, just like you," Melissa had explained.

After she opened her eyes and spotted Liza, she leapt off the deck and ran as fast as she could over to her.

"Hey Liza, me and Emmie are ready! We was so excited that we ate our pancakes super, duper fast." Anna paused. "Why are you hiding in the bushes?"

"Did dad leave yet?" Liza asked in response.

"Yes, I heard his car leaving when I was on the deck." Anna watched as her sister looked at the driveway. "Why ya cryin'?"

Liza quickly wiped her red eyes. "I'm not crying, sport," she said smiling down at Anna. "The wind just blew some dirt in my eyes. You ready to roll?"

"Roll?" Anna asked, confused. "We don't wanna do flips, Liza, we wanna skate."

Liza smiled and tousled Anna's hair. "Of course you do. Come on."

Hand and hand the girls went to the garage to get their skates and pads on.

Melissa walked out the front door a little while later with a steaming cup of coffee and sat down on the cushioned, white porch swing to watch her girls play. Liza was holding Anna's hand, and Emmie's too, Melissa noted with a smile. She was coaching them, shouting words of encouragement and praise to both.

Anna looked over to the porch and waved. "Look, mommy! I'm doing it!" She shouted as she let go of Liza's hand. She skated for about five seconds before her feet got tangled up and she fell.

Liza didn't panic. Instead, she knelt down in front of Anna and said, "Emmie says that was awesome! She says that with just a little bit more practice, you will be a better skater than me!"

Anna looked up at her sister with unshed tears in her eyes. "Do you think so, Liza?"

"I know so. Come on, sport, let's go get some cookies and rest some," Liza said as she untied Anna's skates.

"Did you see us, mommy? We was skating!" Anna exclaimed hopping up the porch steps.

"You were absolutely amazing! Are you sure you've never skated before?" Melissa asked making her way over to open the door for them.

"Yes, mommy," Anna giggled. "Emmie said I might even get better than Liza!"

"That you may." Melissa winked at Liza as they walked into the living room. "Why don't you and Emmie go wash up and we'll set out the milk and cookies."

"Ok." Anna skipped gleefully up the stairs with Emmie held tightly to her chest. "Maybe if we wash up extra good mommy will make us some chocolate milk," she stage whispered to Emmie.

"I'm so proud of you, you know?" Melissa said to Liza as they placed four saucers and four teacups at the table.

Liza's eyebrows knit together. "Why?"

"You are so good to your sister. I know things weren't always easy when you were younger. I'm just happy you guys get along so good and that you love her the way you do."

Shrugging off her mom's complements Liza said, "That's what sister's do, mom. They love, help, and protect each other."

For one split second, Melissa had the most pained expression in her eyes, but she quickly shook it away before Liza could see it. They finished setting out the cookies in silence.

Chapter 3

Someone knocked on the door as the three sat quietly enjoying their Oreos and milk.

"That must be Joey. Daddy has to work late tonight so Joey's going to keep an eye on you until I get home from school." Melissa said, carrying her dishes to the sink.

"Yay!" Anna said as she grabbed Emmie and raced to open the door.

"Mom! I don't need a babysitter. I'm thirteen, not a baby," Liza protested.

"I know you don't need a babysitter, sweetie. But with all the break-ins that have been happening lately, I would just feel better knowing you weren't here alone, so I asked Joey over," Melissa soothed, placing a hand on Liza's shoulder. "Don't be upset. We'll say he's watching the house, not you. How's that sound?"

Liza smiled. "That sounds good. Can I see if Marybeth can come over? Pleeease?"

"That's fine by me, but you girls have to promise to be on your best behavior."

"Promise!" Liza shouted as she took off running for the phone.

Anna had Joey by the hand, pulling him into the kitchen while giving him a non-stop commentary of her day. All the way down to how they dipped their Oreos in their milk for exactly seven seconds, and then ate them in one big bite.

While Anna was delivering her speech, Melissa finished cleaning up the kitchen. As she was walking to her room to change and get her purse and keys, the doorbell rang.

"I got it! I got it!" Liza shouted, running past her mom.

When Melissa returned, she found everyone in the living room. Liza and Marybeth were sitting on the floor playing, what looked to be, an intense game of war. Joey was in the brown, plush recliner, and Anna was at the movie shelf searching for the perfect movie to watch.

"I should be home around four-thirty. I don't want anyone outside, ok?"

"Ok, mom," Liza said without looking up.

"Anna?"

"Ok, Mommy," Anna said. "I love you. Be good at school."

Melissa chuckled. "I will. And I love you, too. Love you, Liza."

Liza looked up then, "Oh, love you too, mom. Bye."

Shaking her head and smiling, Melissa looked at Joey. "Call if you need anything."

"Will do, Mrs. W."

"Can we watch the *SpongeBob Movie*? Please, please, please!" Anna asked as she jumped onto Joey's lap.

"Sure thing, kiddo. I'll go put it in," Joey said as he lifted her off.

"I'll help! I know how!"

Joey snagged her around the waist while Anna was in mid-step. "Why don't you keep my seat warm for me? I don't want it to get cold." He plopped her down onto the chair.

As soon as the movie started playing, Anna had Emmie sitting on her lap two feet away from the television. Joey chuckled and reclaimed his chair.

When *SpongeBob* was halfway over, Anna turned around to see that Liza and Marybeth were nowhere in sight. Holding Emmie by her arm, she walked over to Joey and asked, "Can I sit with you?"

"You sure can, honey." Joey leaned forward, scooped her up, and set her on his lap. Pulling Anna to his chest, he gave her a gentle squeeze. "You are getting so big, you know that?" He whispered into her ear.

Animation lit Anna's eyes as she turned quickly in his lap to face him. "I am. Liza took me outside today and I learned how to skate! Soon I will be the best skater in the whole world!"

Joey smiled and put his face closer to hers and whispered, "And the most beautiful." He kissed her on the nose and turned her around, pulling her snugly back against his chest. He left one arm securely around her waist.

When he saw that Anna was focused on the movie again, he pressed his face to her hair and inhaled deeply. He listened to Liza and Marybeth playing cards behind his chair. He thought himself quite brilliant for suggesting they play back there so that they would not be distracted by the television. It sounded like they had just started a new game of war, which was perfect. That game could last a very long time. Focusing his attention back on Anna, he slowly placed one hand on her knee. He watched her face intently to judge her reaction. She seemed to be completely engulfed in her movie.

He released his grip on her waist just enough to gently slide his hand to the hem of her shirt. He slid his fingers one by one underneath her shirt until his hand was fully inside it. Slowly he moved his hand upwards until he reached her rib cage. He could feel nearly every one of her ribs as he rested it against her small stomach. With his other hand, he started rubbing soft circles on her knee. With each small circle, he let his fingertips slip further and further up her thigh until he was tickling the edge of her short green shorts.

Anna stiffened.

Joey's hand froze, then he let his whole hand relax against her upper thigh. "Shh. It's ok, sweetie. I'm not going to hurt you." He kept his hands still until it seemed that she had relaxed and was focused on the movie again. Then he slowly started caressing her rib cage.

But Anna was not focused on the movie. Not at all. Her tummy wasn't feeling too good now, and her head was a little dizzy. And she was starting to feel scared. Why was she feeling like this? She felt….icky. Like she was doing something very, very wrong. Why was he rubbing her leg like that? And why did he have his hand in her shirt? Her daddy and mommy never touched her like that. Her thoughts had slammed to a halt when she felt his fingers, ever so lightly, start to massage her chest.

"Where's Liza?" She asked in a low, shaky whisper.

"She's behind the chair. Why don't you peak back there and see if her and Marybeth are still playing war?"

Relief swept through Anna when she felt his hands move away from where they had been. She started to jump off his lap when she felt his arms around her again.

"You don't have to get up. Just turn around here on the chair and peak at them. I won't let you fall. Besides, your sister might get mad if you interrupt her game. You don't want to make her mad, do you?" Joey breathed in her ear as he squeezed her gently back against his chest.

Anna couldn't talk, her voice wouldn't work, so she just shook her head and slowly turned around to look at her sister and Marybeth. She longed for her sister to look at her and see that something was not right and tell Anna to come join her to play, but neither girl seemed to notice her. She wished she could tell Joey to stop, that she did not like what he was doing, but she couldn't. Her mommy had always told her to respect her elders. And Joey was older than her, so she had to listen, right?

Once again, Anna's thoughts came to a screeching halt when she felt the hand that Joey had placed on her back start rubbing along-side the upper edge of her shorts. His hand was slowly moving down and was almost to her bottom. Anna stopped breathing when she felt his hand slide over it and stop just past the bottom edge of her shorts.

Stop! Her brain shouted. *This ain't right! I don't like you touching me like that! Please, stop!*

What was he doing? Where he was touching her now made her feel like she was going to use the bathroom on herself. Like he was tickling her, but in a place he was not supposed to be tickling. She hated it, but didn't dare move for fear of what he might do next.

She wanted to weep with relief when he finally moved his hand back down her leg. He gently gave her a tug with the arm that he had against her stomach, turning her back around in the chair. Sitting once again on his lap, she didn't say a word, she barely even breathed. At least he didn't put his hand in her shirt again, she could be happy about that.

Joey leaned his head forward and brushed her neck with soft, quiet kisses. "Did you enjoy that?" He whispered into her ear.

Anna couldn't speak, so she gave her head a quick, small shake.

"Oh. Well, next time we will have to make it more fun for you. How about that?"

Anna didn't answer. Instead, she stared straight ahead, not moving a muscle. Afraid that if she did, he would touch her there again.

"You know you're my favorite girl, right?" Joey glanced at the clock. "Your mom will be getting home soon. I wouldn't tell her about the fun we had. She wouldn't understand and might get mad at you. We don't want that now, do we?" He asked, kissing her neck again.

When Joey finally stopped, Anna did everything she could to make sure she didn't cry. If she did her mommy or her sister might ask what was wrong. But Joey said that if she told them they might get mad at her. She didn't want that. She wanted to get away from Joey, far away, but he had his arms wrapped snugly around her waist. The only thing Anna could think to do was close her eyes and pretend she was not there. Not sitting on Joey's lap, feeling his hands holding on to her.

She was walking in a big open field with Emmie walking next to her. There were beautiful flowers with the brightest colors she had ever seen. The sky was light blue with the sun shining softly in the middle. Just to the right of the sun was a big, brilliant rainbow.

Anna stared at the rainbow in her mind. Her mommy had always told her that a rainbow was God's way to remind His people that He would not forget His promises. She wanted to ask why God had forgotten her. Why He let Joey hurt her like that. But she wouldn't ask, not here in her special place. This place was only for good thoughts and beautiful things.

A Secret Well Kept

Chapter 4

She must have fallen asleep, because the next thing she knew her mommy was gently shaking her shoulder.

"Anna, wake up, baby. It's time for dinner," Melissa whispered as she brushed the hair away from Anna's face.

Slowly, Anna opened her eyes. It took several seconds for them to focus. She was on the couch. Looking over at the chair, she was relieved to see that it was empty. She looked around the room, quickly scanning it to see if Joey was still there. He wasn't. When she finally looked back at her mommy, she lunged into her arms and squeezed tightly.

"Oh! What's wrong, darling? Did you have a bad dream?"

A flashback entered Anna's mind. Joey... in the chair... her in his lap... his hands were... And his voice repeating over and over again, "They'll be mad... They'll be mad... They'll be mad." Anna swallowed the lump that was trying to let her cry out the truth. Slowly she said, "Yes mommy, a very bad dream."

"Well, it's over now. You're awake and mommy's home." Pulling Anna back to look into her eyes Melissa said, "And guess what we are having for dinner?"

Anna didn't answer, only shrugged her shoulders.

"Your absolute favoritist thing in the world! Spaghetti with ginormous meatballs!"

Anna knew her mommy was trying to make her happy so she gave the best smile she could give and tried to look happy.

"Why don't you and Emmie go wash up and meet us in the kitchen?"

"Ok, mommy," Anna said as she picked Emmie up from the couch and walked away.

When she got back, she found her mommy and sister already seated at the table. Liza telling an animated version of the games that she and Marybeth had played. Anna walked quietly over to the table, placed Emmie in her chair and sat down. She watched her mommy's face while she listened to Liza's stories. She looked like she was really happy hearing everything that Liza was saying. Joey said that if she told her mommy what they had played, she would get really mad. Anna did not want her mommy to get mad at her.

As Anna sat there pushing her meatballs back and forth on her plate, she heard Liza telling her mommy about winning almost every game that she and Marybeth had played except for speed. That she only lost that one because Marybeth had been playing that game for years and she had just learned how to play. Liza talked on and on, and for that Anna was grateful. She was way too sad and confused to talk.

"Anna?"

"Huh?" Anna mumbled, glancing up at her mommy.

"I asked how your day was, sweetie," Melissa repeated patiently.

Anna looked away quickly before her mommy could see the truth in her eyes. "It was fine, mommy," she whispered.

Melissa placed her hand softly on Anna's arm. "Anna, honey, are you ok?"

Setting her fork down, she folded her hands in her lap. Barely lifting her head, she replied, "Nothing's wrong, mommy. My tummy just don't feel so good. Can I go lay down?"

"You haven't eaten any of your food yet. Aren't you hungry? It's your favorite." Melissa coaxed. "And we can make brownies for dessert."

Lifting her head a bit more Anna said, "No thank you, mommy. I'm not really hungry. Can I go now, please?"

Melissa gave Liza a questioning look, but Liza just shrugged her shoulders and continued eating.

"Of course, baby. You go ahead and lay down. I'll come check on you in a little while."

Anna and Emmie were out the door before Melissa could even finish the sentence. Melissa stared after her a few seconds longer before she turned her attention back to Liza and hearing about her day.

Anna heard her mommy come into her room later that night after Liza came to bed, but she did not want to talk. Anna laid as still as possible so her mommy would think she was asleep. When she heard the footsteps walking back down the hall, she opened her eyes.

"Should I tell mommy what happened, Emmie? Joey said mommy would get mad." Tears started running down her cheeks as she squeezed Emmie tighter to her chest. "I don't want to make mommy mad, so I won't tell her. And you can't tell her either. Promise me, Emmie." Anna closed her eyes, "Promise me."

Anna heard her door creak a little later and her eyes snapped open. *Oh no!* She thought. *Joey came to play some more! He said he would and now he's walking up to my bed!* Seeing him get closer, she quickly shut her eyes and pretended to sleep. Anna nearly melted with relief when she heard her daddy whispering to Liza. When Liza started climbing down, Anna sat up.

"Where are you going, Liza?"

"Liza is going to come help daddy with a special project. You go on back to sleep now," George said quietly.

"I want to help too, daddy." Anna started to scoot off her bed when she was stopped by her daddy's hand.

"No. You're too little to help right now. Maybe when you get bigger you can."

"But I am bigger. I'm almost seven!" George patted her bottom, "Maybe next time. Now get on back to sleep." With that, he walked to where Liza stood waiting and they left the room, closing the door behind them.

"Why does Liza get to help daddy?" Anna whispered to Emmie. "I can't wait till I'm bigger so I can help too." She kissed Emmie's cheek and struggled to fall back asleep.

A Secret Well Kept

Chapter 5

The next morning, Anna awoke to the sound of muffled cries coming from above her. Carefully she stood on the edge of the mattress and grabbed the side rails of the top bunk.

Peeking her head up, Anna whispered, "Liza, what's wrong?"

The crying ceased and Liza removed the pillow that she had been using to cover her face. Sniffling one last time and wiping the tears from her eyes she replied, "Nothing, shorty, I just had a very bad nightmare. I'm all better now." Liza put a smile on her face. "What do you say we go eat some breakfast and clean up, then we can go practice skating some more?"

That prospect made Anna jump off the bed, scream yes, grab Emmie and go racing from the room.

Tomorrow would be Monday, so if she practiced more today, then she would be way better. Anna could go to school and tell everyone that she learned how to skate better than Liza when her teacher asked what she did over the weekend.

Two weeks later, Anna still was not sleeping well. Every time she closed her eyes she would see herself sitting on Joey's lap, Emmie clutched tightly to her chest. She would feel his hands touching where they should *not* be touching.

Was it my fault? Did I do something that told him I wanted him to do that? Did I want him to? NO! The answer came firm and fast every time that thought crossed her mind. She most definitely did *not* want him touching her there. She did not want him to touch her anywhere, *ever*.

Right then, on that Tuesday night, Anna vowed that she would never let something like that happen again. She would kick, or scream, or bite. Whatever it took, she would never let someone hurt her like that again!

"Mrs. Wright, thank you for coming in." Anna's teacher smiled and extended her hand to Melissa.

"Not a problem, Ms. Adams." Melissa smiled easily. "It's been a while since I came in. I'm glad you called."

Ms. Adams sat down behind her desk and gestured for Melissa to take the chair opposite her. "I'm happy you were able to, I know you have a busy schedule. The reason I asked you to come in is because I'm a little concerned about Anna. Has she seemed... different at home?"

Confused, Melissa shook her head. "No, she's the same Anna she's always been. Why do you ask?"

"She seems a little... withdrawn lately. Not as... I don't know... happy go lucky would be the best phrase, I guess. She hasn't been playing with the other children like she used to. She's not wanting to participate in class either. She is usually the first one to volunteer to help me with anything. Now, however, she just sits at her desk quietly, keeping completely to herself."

Melissa looked at Ms. Adams quizzically. "Please forgive me if I am misunderstanding, but... are you saying that you are concerned because Anna is being quiet? It would seem to me that this is a good thing. Maybe she is finally listening. I have had a million conversations with her about her talking in class. You know how it's been all year. It's good to know she's paying more attention now."

Ms. Adams leaned forward, clasped her hands together and placed her arms on the edge of the desk, her rainbow bangle bracelets rattling a moment before the room fell silent.

"This may come across as a little personal, but has anything happened at home?" When

Melissa started to get out of her seat to challenge her, Ms. Adams quickly held her arms up in front of her, palms facing Melissa. "I don't mean anything bad by that. I simply mean that sometimes the littlest thing can cause a child to withdraw. Any kind of change in life can affect them. Has anything recently changed in your home?"

Melissa took a breath to calm herself. "Of course not," she replied through a false smile. "I don't really think anything is wrong with Anna, but since you were concerned enough to call for this meeting, I'll have a talk with her. Ask her personally if anything is wrong." Standing, she held out her hand and briefly shook Ms. Adams' slightly smaller one. "Again, thank you for your concern for Anna."

"You're very welcome. And please, if there is anything at all that I can do, don't hesitate to call."

Melissa nodded and turned on her heel, leaving without looking back.

"How dare she question me about Anna. Like I wouldn't notice if something was wrong," Melissa muttered to herself as she opened the door of her car. She knew all too well what it was like when there were secrets to hide.

She would absolutely know if her Anna was hiding something. She just knew she would.

A Secret Well Kept

34

Chapter 6

"Who's ready for some ice cream!?!" Melissa asked as she walked through the door.

Anna, who had been sitting on the couch watching *SpongeBob*, jumped up and shouted, "I do! I do!"

"Where's Liza and daddy?" Melissa asked when she noticed they were not in the room.

Anna turned to the chair where her daddy had been sitting. The chair she would never, ever sit in again, but her daddy wasn't there. "I don't know. Liza was watching *SpongeBob* with me, but then daddy said she was 'posed to be doing her reading homework in her room. Liza said she could do it out here by me, but then daddy said she would get distracted and then Liza said no she wouldn't. That's when daddy gave her 'the look', so Liza went to her room. I don't know where daddy went after that 'cause I wasn't watching."

"I'm right here, Melissa," George said as he walked into the room tucking his shirt in. "What do you want?"

Melissa hesitated, "Where's Liza?"

"She was in her room reading when I passed on my way to the bathroom."

"Oh. Ok. Well, I brought some ice cream home for us," Melissa said, still standing by the door.

George looked at his watch. "It will be too late for ice cream by the time you get dinner made. You should have come home sooner."

"I had to meet with Anna's teacher. I thought you would have made them dinner already and we could have had dessert now."

Anna's ears perked up at that. "Why'd you have to talk to Ms. Adams? I didn't get in trouble at school. I even stopped talking too much like you told me."

Melissa walked over to the couch and knelt down. "Of course not, honey. You have been sooo good. We were just talking about--"

"Anna," George interrupted, "go to your room and read with your sister. Mommy and I need to talk. I'll come get you when we're done."

"Ok, daddy." Anna grabbed Emmie from the couch and skipped down the hall but paused in her doorway.

Liza was sitting in the corner with her knees pulled up to her chest and her face buried in her hands. Anna looked back down the hall but couldn't see her mommy or daddy. Quietly, she closed the door, walked over to Liza, and knelt beside her.

"Liza?" Anna put her small hand on Liza's shoulder. Liza stiffened. "Liza, what's wrong? Why are you crying? Did you fall off your bed?"

Liza couldn't answer, instead she just shook her head.

"Did daddy make you cry? He sounded mad when he came back from the bathroom."

Liza jerked her head up and looked first at the door then at Anna. Wiping her face, she said, "No, short stuff. Nothing's wrong. Dad didn't make me cry. Everything's ok."

"Then why were you crying?"

"Nothing. It's nothing. Like I said, everything's fine. You're going to be ok."

Anna looked at Liza confused. "I'm not crying, you are."

Liza put on the best smile she could muster. "Hey French fry, you want to build a castle?"

Anna's eyes lit up. "Yes! ....But how?"

Liza knew that would take Anna's mind off her tears. She meant what she said too, Anna would be okay. Liza would make sure of it.

"Simple," Liza said as she jumped up and grabbed the blankets off the bed.

For the next hour, Anna and Liza stayed in their room building their castle.

"Knock, knock," Melissa said as she opened the girls' bedroom door.

"Halt! Who goes there?" Anna commanded.

"Um….Mommy. Can I come in?"

"What's the magic word?" Anna asked in her most serious voice.

"…Please?"

"No!"

"Pretty please?"

"Nope!"

"Hocus Pocus? …Open Sesame?"

The girls laughed from inside their makeshift castle.

"That's not it either," Liza said.

"Give me a hint?" Melissa asked smiling.

"Me and you and Anna."

"Umm...Girls?"

"And what do girls do?"

"….Ok, I'm stumped. What do girls do?"

"We rule!" Anna said jumping out of the castle.

"We do? And what do boys do?" Melissa chuckled.

"They leave us alone." Liza mumbled as she came out.

Melissa looked at her and her smile dropped. "Why do you say that? Has some boy been messing with you at school? If he is, you know you can tell me. I will go and talk to the principal about it. I won't let anyone bother my babies."

Liza looked at Melissa, then at Anna and back to Melissa again. "No, mom. Nobody is bothering me. We were just being silly."

Melissa stared at Liza for a few more seconds. "Ok, but remember what I said. Both of you," she said as she looked at Anna. "If anyone bothers you, or tries to do things you don't want them to do, you can tell me."

"We know mommy. We was just having fun and talking about silly boys, that's all." Anna said. "Do we get ice cream-- Mommy, was you crying? Your eyes are all red. And you got a big red spot on your face. Did you get hurt?" Melissa's eyes opened wide for the briefest moment and her hand reflexively covered her cheek. She quickly schooled her expression and said, "No, honey, I'm not hurt. I just tripped coming down the hall and hit the wall. You know how clumsy mommy is."

"Can we get some ice cream then?" Anna asked.

Melissa took a quick glance back before answering, "Not tonight honey. Daddy's right, it will be way too late to eat ice cream after we eat dinner. I made meatloaf and potatoes. Let's go eat, then we can get ready for bed, ok?"

"Ok," Anna replied sadly before an idea came to her. "Can we have ice cream tomorrow night then?"

Melissa smiled down at Anna, "If you promise to be good at school tomorrow and do all of your homework, we can. Deal?" Melissa held her hand out to Anna.

Rushing quickly over to her mom she grabbed her hand and shook it. "Deal."

Chapter 7

Two weeks later, Anna cuddled up next to Emmie after having the best time on the field trip to the zoo with her class. Ms. Adams even told her how happy she was that Anna was acting like her old self again.

"But Ms. Adams, I'm only six, that's not old," *Anna had said to her teacher.*

Ms. Adams had chuckled and squatted down to Anna's eye level and told her she meant that she was glad Anna was happy and smiling again. She had said that the last couple of weeks Anna seemed to have been upset or sad about something. She was glad to see that Anna was doing better.

"But I'm not really all better, Emmie. I still get scared when I think about Joey. I don't want him to come back. Never, ever again."

Anna stopped talking when her door opened, and Liza walked in. She was glad that she wasn't facing the door so she could wipe her eyes before Liza saw her crying because she would ask what was wrong. But she wasn't allowed to tell. Joey had said that if she told them, her mommy and Liza would get mad. Anna couldn't tell anyone, except for Emmie. She watched the outline of Liza as she got ready for bed. She couldn't wait until she was older like Liza. She would be strong and brave and never let anyone hurt her.

"Ouch!" Liza whispered as she was pulling her shirt over her head.

Anna sat up. "Are you ok?"

Liza quickly covered her side with her shirt, thankful for the dark. "Nothing's wrong, sport. I just had a muscle ache. It's gone now. You should get back to sleep, 'cause we are practicing skating again tomorrow and you need to be rested so you're not too tired after school."

Anna looked at Liza a moment longer before agreeing and laying back down.

"Good night, Liza. I love you."

"Good night, Anna. Love you too." Under her breath, Liza added, "More than you will ever know."

After changing, Liza made sure Anna wasn't looking before she opened the closet door and quietly got out her journal. She grabbed the book light from her dresser, climbed up to the top bunk and started writing.

Anna was glad when school was over the next day. She could barely sit still in class; she was so excited to practice skating with Liza again. As soon as she got home, she raced off the bus and into the house. She couldn't wait for Liza to get there so they could start. She ran straight to her room, changed out of her school clothes, got her skates ready and grabbed Emmie off her bed. As she was going back downstairs, she heard her mommy on the phone in the kitchen. She started to go in there for a snack, but when she heard what her mommy was saying she froze, and all the blood drained from her face.

"...you sure you don't mind coming over and keeping an eye on the girls for me? ...Liza's friend, Marybeth, is supposed to come over and spend the night. Would that be ok, too? ...Thank you so much. George was supposed to be home early today, but he just called and said he had to call a last-minute meeting about some case he's working on and won't be home 'til around ten. I usually leave at 4:30, could you be here by then? ...Great! Thanks again. See you shortly."

Anna couldn't breathe. Joey was coming. He said that he would be back to "play", and now he was coming. Anna turned around and as fast and quietly as she could, ran back to her room. She didn't want to skate anymore. She didn't want to do anything except hide. She definitely did *not* want her mommy to leave. She didn't like

Joey's games, they made her feel scared. She curled up on the bed and covered her head with the blanket. This couldn't be happening. Joey was coming back for her. Tears started running down her face as she tried to pray that he wouldn't come, that she wouldn't have to play any more of his games. She must have fallen asleep praying, because the next thing she knew Liza was shaking her shoulder.

"Hey, jellybean, wake up. I thought we were going to skate today. This morning you said you'd be ready and that you would skate even better this time. You ready to go?"

Anna looked up at her sister, trying to hide her sadness. She wished she could tell her that no, she wasn't ready. That she would never be ready when Joey was coming over. But she knew she couldn't tell anyone about that, so she said the only thing she could think of.

"I don't think I can today. I have a tummy ache. I might need to stay in bed all night."

Liza furled her brow and sat on the bed next to Anna. "Are you ok? Did you eat something at lunch that your tummy didn't like? Remember that time you drank too much milk and your tummy got upset? Did you drink too much milk at school?"

Anna just shook her head.

"Ok. I'll let mom know that you don't feel good. She told me that Jimmy was coming over to watch us since dad is working late. I'll tell him that you don't feel good and are staying in your room. I'll come check on you in a little while. Do you need some water?"

Anna's eyes went wide. *Jimmy was coming? Not Joey?* Maybe her prayers had worked.

"But...but I thought Joey was coming."

"I thought mom told you. Joey had to move because he got a new job somewhere. He came by the other night to say bye, but you were already in bed."

"Really?" Anna tried to keep the excitement out of her voice. Never before had she been glad that she had to go to bed an hour before Liza. Now, however, she was extremely grateful. She didn't have to see Joey, and, if Liza was right, would never have to play his games again. She hardly dared to hope it was the truth.

"Yep. I know you're probably sad, you liked him a lot."

Anna knew she couldn't vocally agree with that statement without her voice betraying her, so she just nodded her head. Then she asked, "Liza, who's Jimmy?"

Liza smiled. "He's our cousin. You probably don't remember him but I knew him forever. He's fun. He always comes up with the best games."

Anna almost stopped breathing again. *Best games? Like the kind of games Joey played?* But no, that couldn't be. Liza wouldn't like him if he played games like that. He must play real games.

"Liza, I think my tummy is feeling better. Can we still skate?"

Standing, she pulled Anna off the bed and threw her arm around her. "Of course we can, sprite. It's 3:30 right now, so we have about forty-five minutes to practice before Marybeth and Jimmy get here. That's plenty of time for you to skate better than me."

Chapter 8

Anna and Liza had just sat down on the porch steps and were taking their skates off when a man started walking up the walkway. Anna tried to scoot closer to Liza, but she had jumped up and ran to the stranger.

"Hey, Jimmy!" Liza opened her arms and gave him a big hug.

So, this is Jimmy. He looks nice. And Liza gave him a hug so he must be good. Anna thought to herself, still sitting and watching.

The stranger walked up to her and smiled. "Look at you! You've grown up so much. The last time I saw you, you were knee high to a grasshopper."

"What? I don't 'member ever being small as a grasshopper," Anna said matter-of-factly.

Jimmy just laughed and ruffled her hair as he walked past her and into the house with Liza. Anna, refusing to be ignored, jumped up and followed him in.

"Hey, what do you mean I was shorter than a grasshopper? I was never that short. Why did you say that?"

Jimmy stopped in the living room while Liza went to tell her mom that he was here.

Squatting down he said, "It just means that you've grown up a lot since the last time I saw you."

"When was the last time you saw me? 'Cause I been this big for a whole year."

"Well, it *has* been a while. It was at the family reunion a couple summers ago. I just moved back to town a few weeks ago."

"Well, I don't remember you," Anna stated.

"That's because at that family reunion you ate too many brownies, before anyone even got there, and gave yourself a tummy ache. You slept most of the day," Melissa said walking up to Jimmy and giving him a hug. "Hey, little Jimmy, how was the move?"

"Aunt Missy, nobody calls me that anymore," Jimmy replied. "The move went good. Had a few issues with the car, but I made it here safe."

"Well, I'm glad you're safe. How's it feel being back at the house? I know your dad's happy you're back. I've heard him on the phone with George and he has done nothing but complain about how far away you were."

"I'm happy to be home again. Mom had my room ready for me. Dad showed me some plans to renovate the house and I can't wait to start on them. I can finally put to use some of the things I learned at school," Jimmy said winking at Liza.

"Ha, Ha. I remember the talk you gave me last time about school. You don't need to remind me. I am taking it more seriously this year, you can ask my mom. I haven't had anything below a B so far. No more C's for me. Promise," Liza said as she made an "X" over her heart.

Melissa bent over and kissed Liza on the head. "That's good, because if you ever want to succeed in life you have to--"

"Do good in school." Liza and Anna said in unison.

"OK, my smart girls, no more lecturing from me. I've got to get to school now myself. Jimmy, I ordered pizza for dinner and the money's on the fridge. Text me if you need anything and I'll answer when I can," Melissa said heading towards the door.

"No worries, Aunt Missy, we'll be fine. You go and have fun at school."

"Love you, girls."

"Love you!" they yelled together.

Liza, Marybeth, Anna, and Jimmy had just finished eating their pizza when Liza suggested they play a game.

"I know a game we could play. It's called cats and dogs. Ever play it?" Jimmy asked.

"No." Liza looked at Marybeth who shook her head.

"What about you, Anna? You ever play cats and dogs?"

"Nope. How do you play it?"

Jimmy put his elbows on the table and leaned in. "It's simple. Cats and dogs don't like each other, right?"

All three girls nodded.

"So, to play, you divide up into two teams, one team is the cats, and the other team is the dogs. The dogs have to try and find all the cats."

"That don't sound hard," Anna said.

"Here's the catch, you have to do it where it's dark, so you can't see where anyone is."

"I don't like the dark," Anna pouted.

"Then you can be on my team. We can be the dogs and Liza and Marybeth can be the cats. Liza, where can we play that it can be really dark?"

"Downstairs!" Liza exclaimed, jumping up and running for the basement door with Marybeth right behind her.

When Jimmy and Anna made it down the stairs, Liza and Marybeth were nowhere in sight.

"Liza?" Anna called out. "Where are you?"

"We're hiding," Marybeth answered.

"Come and find us you mangy dogs!" Liza added.

"Ok, you ready? I bet we can sniff them out easily," Jimmy said grabbing Anna's hand then turning out the lights.

Liza was right, you couldn't see your hand in front of your face it was so dark. Jimmy started to pull Anna towards the wall across from the steps. Before he had turned the lights off, he had made sure to catalog everything in the room, where and what everything was, what was on the floors, the best places to hide.

"It's really, really dark. I don't like it this dark," Anna complained. "Can't we just go watch a movie?"

Jimmy pulled Anna closer to his side. "It'll be fun. You'll see, you will love this game. Now, let's go and see if we can find those cats."

They had only been looking for a couple of minutes when Jimmy stopped Anna at the sofa in the far corner. "Let's sit down here, be extra quiet, and see if we can hear them moving around," Jimmy whispered.

"Okay, but Liza is really good at hiding. I can never find her when we play hide and seek." Anna sat down on the couch and tried to listen. After a few seconds she whispered, "I don't hear anything."

Pulling her a little closer, Jimmy said, "Maybe if we try getting on the floor we can."

"How?"

"If we're closer to the ground, we can hear them better when they walk."

That made sense to Anna, so she agreed. They slipped off the couch and got down on their hands and knees.

"Now we're like real dogs," Anna said and started panting like a dog and crawling around.

"Hey, puppy, where are you at? I can't see you." Jimmy moved his hand out and around, searching until he found hers. "Oh, there you are. Come here and I'll show you something funny." Jimmy tugged Anna towards him. As he did, he let go of her hand and put his arm around her waist. "You gotta be really close so I can show you," Jimmy whispered.

When Anna felt his arm around her waist, she froze. She didn't like the way his arm around her made her feel. It made her remember what Joey did, and she really didn't like to remember that.

"Do you know how dogs use the bathroom?"

Anna was silent, too scared to answer.

"Hey, are you still awake? Did you fall asleep standing up like the cows do?" Jimmy chuckled.

OK, see. It's not like Joey. He's just trying to be silly and play the game. Don't think about Joey, don't think about Joey, Anna told herself. It was not the first time she had to tell herself this. Ever since *that* happened, she didn't like when any man got close to her. But this was her cousin. Someone in her family would never hurt her like that.

"I know how they use the potty. Everyone does," Anna said.

"Prove it," Jimmy whispered.

Anna frowned. "How can I show you? It's too dark to see."

"Easy." Jimmy gently squeezed Anna's waist. "You know how blind people use their hands to see? I'll pretend I'm blind and use my hands to feel what you're doing." He started sliding his hand over her hip and down her leg to her thigh. "Ok. Show me how dogs use the bathroom."

Anna didn't move. She couldn't breathe. *No, no, no* was all her mind could think.

"Are you still awake?" Jimmy asked tickling her leg.

Since Anna was extremely ticklish, she couldn't help but laugh. It calmed her down enough to answer. "They lift their leg like this." Anna lifted her leg to the side.

Jimmy moved his hand back to Anna's side and gave her another little tickle. "That's right. That is how *boy* dogs use the bathroom. But do you know how girl dogs do?"

"Of course I know that. I *am* six, you know?"

Anna showed him by opening her knees and dropping her bottom towards the ground. "Like this."

"Perfect," Jimmy whispered.

As she started to get back up, she felt Jimmy's hand push down gently on her bottom. Anna stopped breathing. *What is he doing? We were playing a game, but now this don't feel right. Maybe it's just too dark and he can't see where his hand is at.*

All these thoughts were swirling in Anna's head when Jimmy got close to her ear and whispered, "Let me ask you another question. Do you know where it comes from when they use the bathroom?"

Anna tried to answer. Tried to tell him that she didn't like where his hand was but couldn't find her voice.

"No? Let me show you." Jimmy moved his hand lower and started rubbing her very private area. "Right here," Jimmy whispered in her ear. "This is where the girl dogs use the bathroom."

Jimmy continued rubbing her. "Do you like this game? I hope you do, 'cause we can play again. Then I can teach you other things that dogs do."

Anna was too afraid to say anything. She remembered how Joey said that if she told anyone, they would all get mad. She loved her family and never, ever wanted to make them mad. So instead of answering, Anna tried to think of all the things that made her happy. *Rainbows. Butterflies. Stars. Mommy. Daddy. Liza. Emmie.*

It felt to Anna like they had been "playing" the game for hours and hours when she finally heard a noise other than the pounding of her own heart. She almost wept for joy when the sound made Jimmy pull his hand away from her.

"Cats rule! Do you give up on finding us?" Liza hollered.

"Never! We will find you, just you wait!" Jimmy shouted back. To Anna he whispered, "Let's not tell them about how we play the game.

They might get mad that they didn't get to play too, ok?"

Anna didn't think they would want to play that way. But what if they did get mad? She didn't want Liza to be mad at her. This would have to be another secret that she could only tell Emmie. She nearly sighed with relief when Jimmy started to move around and really start looking for them.

Chapter 9

"Brush your teeth and get to bed," George said after he saw Jimmy out.

"Will you tuck us in, daddy?" Anna asked.

"Not tonight, I have too much work to do."

"Ok. Love you, daddy. Good night." Anna walked over and gave him a hug while Liza stood in the doorway to the hall watching.

"Liza?" Anna asked after they had brushed their teeth and were lying in bed.

"Yeah?"

"Do you ever get scared of stuff?"

Liza leaned over from the top bunk and looked at Anna. "I get scared sometimes. Why?"

"What do you get scared of?"

"Well, I get scared when my teacher makes me stand up in front of the class and talk, or when I am playing outside and a really big spider gets too close. Why'd you ask?"

"No reason. Good night. Love you." Anna whispered and turned over, hugging Emmie as tight as she could. Liza didn't get scared like her. Liza got scared of the *real* things, but she only got scared of things she only thought *could* happen. One day she would be brave like Liza.

Anna tried to stay awake until Liza was asleep so she could tell Emmie how horribly bad her day was when she heard her door open. She stopped breathing. *There goes my stupid being scared*, Anna thought. But she couldn't help it. What if Joey didn't really leave? What if Jimmy came back after she went to bed? What if they wanted to play their games again? She relaxed, though, when she heard her daddy's voice.

"Liza… Liza, wake up." George whispered. "Liza, get up and help me."

"I can't, I have a test tomorrow," Liza whispered back.

"Get up and help me," he said in the voice that Anna had heard him use with her mommy. The voice that meant you better do what he says or else you will be in big trouble. You might even get a spanking.

Reluctantly, Liza climbed off the bed and they walked out the door closing it quietly behind them.

Anna didn't know why daddy always chose Liza to help him. She would love it if daddy chose her, then maybe she could stop being afraid. She hugged Emmie tighter to her chest and unloaded her misery.

"It happened again. I said that I wouldn't let anything like that happen again, but I did.

Joey moved away, so I thought I would be safe. I thought it would never happen again. But then my cousin Jimmy came over. He said we was playing a game, but we wasn't. He did what Joey did. I hate it. I wish I could tell Liza, or anybody, but he said that I can't because they might get mad, just the same as Joey said. If they both said it, then maybe it's right. Maybe I can't ever tell anybody or else they will get mad." She turned Emmie to face her. "Emmie, do you think I did something wrong? Was I a bad girl and that's why Jimmy hurt me like Joey? I am going to be the best girl from now on. I won't run down the steps or tell mommy made-up stories anymore. I will do everything I am supposed to and won't be bad ever again." She kissed her doll's head. "Good night, Emmie. I love you."

Chapter 10

"Summer break's almost over and you know what that means, right?" Melissa asked the girls as they were walking back from the park. "School! Third grade!" Anna answered, jumping up and down.

Liza, who was walking on the other side of Anna, smiled over at her sister.

"Not only that. What do we do every year right before school starts?" Melissa winked at Liza and looked back at Anna.

"Shopping?" Anna asked.

"No, silly… Ok, well that too. But I'm talking about our yearly camping trip!"

Anna stopped walking and her eyes opened wide. "The one where we get to walk in the woods and swim under the waterfall?"

"That's the one," Melissa smiled at her.

"Yay!" Anna exclaimed as she tugged on her sister's hand. "It's going to be so fun! I want to climb the biggest tree, and since I'm bigger I might get to swing off the rope into the water! Ain't you excited, Liza?"

Liza had almost forgotten about that. She didn't want to go this year, or any other year.

"Yeah, French fry, I'm excited." She forced a smile for her sister's benefit, but inside she was crying.

"We have to pack when we get home because we are leaving early in the morning so that we have the whole weekend," Melissa told them.

Anna squeezed Liza's hand. "We're going to have super lots of fun, ain't we?"

Liza put on the best smile she could and said, "We sure are."

Melissa looked at her oldest daughter and tried to see what was going on in her head. She had always loved the camping trips, but it seemed like she wasn't as excited as she usually was. Thinking back, she recalled that last year she had been a little reluctant to go, also. Maybe she thought that she was too old to enjoy the outdoors. That was probably it.

"The cabin is so big!" Anna exclaimed as she took Emmie on a tour. "If we stand on the porch, we can see forever." She was on her way to show her the view when the doorbell rang.

"That must be Robert," George said coming out of his bedroom. "I invited him to join us."

"George, this is supposed to be our family vacation. Some time that we can spend together without the rush of everyday life." Melissa closed the door as she followed him out.

He stopped and turned on her, giving her a meaningful look. "And he *is* family. We wouldn't want to make him feel unwanted, now would we?"

Melissa looked quickly at the floor and whispered, "No, of course not."

"Good. Now go answer the door while I get a drink."

Placing as big a smile on her face as she could muster, she turned around and walked quickly over and opened the door. "Hello, Robert. Good to see you," she said, giving him a quick hug.

"Hey'a Mis'. How you been?"

"We've been great." Looking around Melissa asked, "Where's Pam?"

Robert's cheeks heated slightly before he answered. "She, uh, she left me. Last night. She just came out and said she didn't want to be with me anymore."

Melissa pulled him into another hug. "Oh no. I am so sorry. You come in and let's not talk about that anymore. You gonna be ok?"

"Yeah," Robert replied as he hugged her back. "Jimmy decided to go with her to help out, so being around family will help. Speaking of, where's those two angels of yours?" As soon as he entered the living room, he was taken hostage by two sets of arms.

"Uncle Robert! I didn't know you were coming!" Liza exclaimed.

At the same time, Anna was saying, "Bet you can't toss me in the air anymore, I'm bigger now!"

"Robert, glad you could make it." George and his brother shared a handshake. "How are you doing?"

"I'm good." Looking at the people around him, he smiled. "Better now."

"Good. Have you had dinner? We were just about to eat."

"I'm famished."

"Sit by me!" Anna said tugging on his arm.

"Ok, Ok." Robert winked at her. "I would be honored to sit by one of the prettiest princesses in the world."

"Hey!" Liza bumped his arm.

"I would love to sit by the *two* most beautiful princesses in the *galaxy*." He chuckled.

Dinner had just finished, and Melissa was cleaning up when George's phone rang.

"Hello...What? How could that have happened?... I had the paperwork in order. All you had to do was file it... Fine. I'll be there to take care of it... No, you don't need to stay, I'll take care of it... Yes, I'm sure. Good night."

Melissa tried to make it seem like she wasn't listening to his conversation, so when he said her name, she simply said, "Hmm?"

"Melissa, I am speaking to you," George said.

She turned around quickly. "Yes?"

"We need to leave right away. I have to take care of some things at the office."

"But...but George, it's our vacation weekend. Can't you just do it on Monday? Or can your secretary do it?"

"No," he said as he stood up. "It can*not* wait. And *no*, she cannot. I have court first thing Monday morning and I need to get it finished."

Melissa did not want to argue so she acquiesced. "Ok. I'll tell the girls that you had to get some work done. They'll understand. Maybe I'll just take them swimming tomorrow instead of hiking."

"No, Melissa. You didn't hear me. I said *we* need to leave right away."

"I can't help at the office. And I don't want to make the girls leave. They look forward to this trip every year. I will explain--"

George stepped closer to her and lowered his voice. "I am *not* leaving you here alone with another man for the weekend. My brother or not, I will not have it. You *will* come home with me. We will ask Robert to stay with the girls and bring them home Sunday morning."

"Robert? He is going through a hard-enough situation. We can't ask him to watch the girls."

"We can and we will. It will do him good."

Ending the conversation, George walked to his bedroom and started packing, knowing that Melissa would talk to Robert and the girls to work out the details.

Chapter 11

"Hey! How was your weekend?" Melissa asked as she rushed out to hug the girls. She was glad when Robert said that keeping the girls would help *him* more than them. It made her feel less guilty for leaving them when it was supposed to be their weekend.

"Awesome!" Liza exclaimed. "We swam the entire day yesterday. We went hiking and saw a bear with two cubs. It was great!"

"How 'bout you? Did you have as much fun as your sister?" Melissa winked at Liza before turning to Anna.

Not sure how to answer, Anna merely nodded. It took everything she had within her not to cringe when she felt a strong hand clasp her shoulder.

"She had a great time," Robert said as he walked up. "We even went canoeing."

Melissa tickled Anna. "Sounds like you did have a great time! I wish I would have been able to stay, but daddy needed my help."

After she stopped laughing Anna replied without making eye contact. "It was fine. I think I just swam too much 'cause now my tummy's hurting and I'm really tired. Can I lay down for a while?"

Concerned, Melissa felt her head. "You don't have a fever, but if your tummy is hurting, of course you can go lay down. Mommy will be up shortly to check on you."

Anna was happy when she was allowed to walk away. She didn't know how much longer she could have stood there. She had made it to the steps when her mom stopped her.

"Hey, hey. Don't you think you're forgetting something?"

"Huh?"

"Um, don't you think you should give your Uncle Robert a hug and thank him for keeping you girls this weekend?"

Her eyes shot up and met his for a split second before she looked down, said yes, and ran over to give him a quick hug. Or at least she wanted it to be quick. He held on a little too long for her liking.

"Thank you for keeping us this weekend," she mumbled without looking at him.

"You are very welcome." Looking over at Liza he said, "We did have a great time, didn't we?"

"We sure did. You should come every year."

Anna did not even want to consider that. She would be happy if she never had to see him again.

"We'd have to talk to your parents about that, but I sure wouldn't mind." Robert smiled over at Melissa.

"We'll see. Anna, you can go ahead and lay down and I'll come check on you after a while."

That was all Anna needed to hear before she hurried down the hall to her room.

She wouldn't cry. Not yet. Not when her mommy, sister or daddy could come in to check on her. No, she couldn't cry right now. But tonight, when everyone was asleep, that's when she would let it all out. She would tell Emmie all about her weekend. She would get it all out so that she could focus on school tomorrow. She should be excited; she would be in the third grade, she loved school, loved her teachers. But she couldn't muster the enthusiasm she usually had. This trip was the exact opposite of what it should have been. And now she didn't think she ever wanted to go again. She would just lay here and wait for her sister to come in and go to sleep.

"Wake up, girls. It's time to get ready for school," Melissa said as she gently shook first Liza's, then Anna's shoulder.

"I'm fine. My tummy doesn't hurt anymore. Love you, goodnight," Anna said turning over.

"Hey, silly. It's morning time, the first day of school. You have to wake up now."

Anna sat straight up. "Morning? Already?"

Liza jumped down from her bunk. "Yep. Time to get ready for a brand-new year. Tenth grade for me and... first grade for you?"

"No way! I am older than that now! I'm in third grade and you know it," Anna declared as she, too, climbed out of bed.

Liza ruffled her hair and said, "I know, shorty. I was just messin' with ya."

Anna swatted at her sister's hand. "Hey! Don't do that, you'll mess my hair up. I gotta look good for school."

Liza laughed as she walked out the bedroom door.

"Bye, Emmie," Anna said as she leaned over her bed. "I didn't get to tell you about this weekend, but I will tonight before bed. Love you. Wish me luck at school."

With that, she walked out to get ready.

Chapter 12

"Ok, students, let's take our seats," Mrs. Prendergast said as she shuffled the remaining students in from the playground. "We had a great time at recess, now let's finish the day just as great!"

Anna walked quickly to her seat, giggling with her new friend, Lilly. She was really liking her new class. She learned that Lilly had just moved there from Washington. Anna thought that was really neat because she had never lived anywhere else. She would love to move away; then maybe bad things wouldn't happen.

"Ok, so now we're going to change it up a little bit and talk about some of the extra guidelines I would like for us all to follow." Walking around to the front of her desk she said, "I only have a few things that I would really like to stress, and they all have to do with how we treat each other. First, always," looking around to meet everyone's eyes she continued, "*always* say please and thank you. I cannot tell you enough how important this is. Not only does it show that you don't just expect things to come to you, but using these words also shows that you appreciate the other person. And sometimes, that one nice thing you say will be the only nice thing that person hears all day. Second, be respectful to others in all things. If someone asks a question that you think is silly, do not, by any means, laugh. The only silly question in here is the one you don't ask. We do not make fun of anyone, no matter what. And lastly, forgive each other. Forgiveness is one of the greatest gifts you can give someone, and it doesn't cost you a penny. If someone apologizes for something, like accidently stepping on your foot in line or bumping into you in the hall, don't be mad at them or be mean. Forgive them, tell them it's ok. If you do these things, we will all get along fabulously! Now, let's get out our math books and turn to page fifteen."

Liza met Anna after school to walk home. "Hey, French fry. How was school?"

Anna's eyes were as bright as her smile when she said, "It was amazing! My teacher is the nicest teacher there ever was! She gives us pieces of candy when we answer questions right. And I met a new friend. Her name is Lilly. She's from Washington. She's really pretty and funny. And we had gym today, that was really fun! We got to play jump rope and four square! I can't wait till tomorrow 'cause we get to go to art class. I think that will be even more fun…"

As Anna talked on, Liza thought back to her third-grade year. She could remember how carefree her life was. Her mom was pregnant with her sister, she was really good in school, and her dad was still her dad. What she wouldn't give to go back to those happier days. Maybe one day things would be better, she hoped.

When they got to the house, Melissa had a snack of apple slices and peanut butter prepared for them in the kitchen, where they all sat and told about their day. This was a tradition that she started when Liza was still in elementary. She wanted to make sure her girls knew that they were important. That no matter what else was going on, she would stop and listen to whatever they had to say. So they all sat around having a great time and telling each other little things they liked or found funny throughout the day.

Dinner that evening, however, was a completely different atmosphere. Gone was the twinkle in her eyes as she laughed and the easy bantering from earlier. George had gotten into the habit of working through the dinner hour, so it was usually just her and the girls, but not tonight. Melissa hated that she had started getting quieter when he was home. She hated the fact that he belittled her, especially in front of the girls. She *really* hated that despite her pain, she still loved him. She just wished he could be the man he was when they first met. He used to be so attentive to her and the girls. He used to laugh and joke with her and make her feel like a princess. Now he just made her feel like a failure. But she wouldn't give up hope. Hope that one day he would return to his old self, if not for her, then for the girls.

That night after she made sure her sister was asleep, Anna looked into Emmie's eyes. "I didn't get to tell you about this weekend since I fell asleep so fast yesterday. But now I'm thinking maybe I shouldn't. My teacher talked about special rules. They're probly just for class, but they make a lot of sense for the rest of the time too. She says that if someone says they're sorry, then we should forgive them. And after what happened this weekend, he did say sorry. So, I should forgive him, right?" She turned over to her back and stared up at Liza's bed. "When I do mean things to Liza, and I say I'm sorry, I want her to forgive me. So, shouldn't I do the same thing? It's very hard, but I think I should. At least, I'm going to try. And that means that I probly shouldn't talk about it, huh?" Letting out a deep sigh, Anna laid there and thought more about what forgiving someone meant. Did it mean that you like them again? That you trust them again? She decided that forgiving is tricky, but she would try.

Chapter 13

The rest of the school year went great. Anna made new friends, Liza made new friends, and Melissa graduated nursing school. The only thing that would have made the year better in Melissa's eyes would have been if George had been more involved. It seemed to her that he was away from them more than not. He even had several weekend trips that he insisted he must go on. If not for the girls, she didn't think she would have made it through. They gave her a reason to keep going, although she dreaded the weekends when both George and the girls were gone. Sometimes while he was out of town, the girls would ask to go to their friends' houses for a night or two. Those times were the hardest for her. She barely wanted to get up in the morning, let alone get dressed. More often than not she would just sit in her robe and watch TV. It was on one of these mornings at the beginning of summer that George surprised her and came home early.

Melissa was cuddled up in her soft, terry cloth robe watching *Wheel of Fortune* when George strode purposely through the door. Her eyes lit up, she got up and rushed towards him.

"George, what a surprise! I didn't expect you home until tomorrow."

"Where are the girls?" He asked looking past her around the room.

"They're…" Melissa shook her head slightly, getting her thoughts together. "Liza is at Marybeth's house and Anna is at Lilly's."

He walked past her to the dining room. "I suppose that's for the best. Come in here, we need to talk."

Melissa was hesitant. He hadn't really had a conversation with her in months. Honestly, it seemed as though he completely ignored her as of late. She didn't want him to get angry, though, so she quickly hurried to sit at the table, not saying a word, just looking at him.

"I want a divorce."

Melissa reeled back. "What? I don't understand. What do you mean? Why?" She couldn't get her thoughts straight.

"Come now. Don't act like you didn't see this coming."

She got up and started pacing the floor. "But… but the girls. Our life." She looked up at him. "We can make this work. We love each other--"

"No. I do not love you," he interrupted. "I have not loved you for a while now. I stayed as long as I have thinking it could work, but it isn't."

Melissa kneeled in front of him. "But it could. We could make it work. We can't give up on us. I'll try harder. I know we--"

George stood abruptly and walked to the sink. "NO. There is no making this work, and there is no us. There hasn't been for years now. I've already had the paperwork drawn up. You can have the house and the car. As long as you live here, you can have custody of the girls, I will get them every other weekend and alternating holidays. You have your nursing degree now, so you should be able to support them."

Tears were falling down Melissa's cheeks as she stood up and walked closer to him. "George, please. We can't do this. The girls need their parents. They need us to be together. Just tell me what I've got to do and I'll do it."

He grabbed her arms. "You're not listening. This is not open for debate." He released her long enough to pull an envelope from his jacket pocket. "I've already signed them. Sign them while I go pack and I'll file them Monday." He dropped the papers on the table as he walked past her and to their room.

Melissa could hardly breathe. All she wanted was to give her girls the kind of family that she didn't have when she was a kid. How could he turn his back on them? What was she going to tell her girls? These thoughts were running through her head as she sat at the table, just staring at the paper.

"Are you finished?" George asked when he walked back in. Looking over at her he sighed and sat down at the table. "Look, this is how it is. You either sign the papers right now and take what I've offered, or I will take you to court, take the house, the car and full custody of the girls. This is happening; how it happens is up to you." He placed a pen on the table beside the papers and stared at her.

She looked back with tear filled eyes. She knew he would win if they went to court. What other choice did she have really? Slowly she picked up the pen, opened the papers and signed them. Sliding them across the table, she couldn't look up. She continued looking at the table long after the door shut behind him.

"Mom, I'm home. You should have seen me last night. Marybeth's mom took us to the skate rink. They had some races there and I came in second place! Then when we got back, we stayed up watching all the *Harry Potter* movies and eating cookies. It was so fun. You should have seen Marybeth when we woke up this-- Mom? Are you ok?" Liza asked when she saw her mom sitting at the dining room table, her eyes puffy and red.

Melissa took a moment to gather herself before saying, "I will be." She looked up at Liza and said, "Come sit. I want to talk to you about daddy before Anna gets home." She patted the chair next to her.

Liza slowly walked over and sat. *Did she know? What did he tell her? What was she going to do?* were the questions racing through her head. "What's going on?" was all she asked.

"I need to tell you something, but I want you to know that none of this is your fault. And we will get through this, ok?"

"Ok..."

"Daddy and I had a long talk yesterday; we are going to be making some changes." Melissa took a breath trying to figure out how best to say what she needed to say.

Liza held her breath. She just knew that he had told her mom. What was she going to do? Did she blame her like he said she would?

"Daddy and I are getting a divorce," she blurted out.

Liza had not expected her to say *that.* "What?"

"I know it's hard. And it's ok to be sad. I want you to know that we both love you kids a whole bunch, and that, no matter what, we will be here for you."

This was the absolute best news she had heard in a long time. *He was leaving-- wait, he was leaving, right?* She opened her mouth to ask, but her mom beat her to it.

"Daddy is going to move out and we are staying here. You girls don't have to leave your friends or school."

Even better!

"But don't worry, you will still get to see daddy. Every other weekend, you girls will go over to daddy's to spend the weekend with him."

What? She did *not* want to go over there. *Ever.*

Mistaking her silence for sadness, Melissa moved to wrap her arms around Liza. "It will be ok, I promise. We will be ok." She held her tight for a couple of minutes when they heard the door open. She hesitated a moment before letting go and turning to face Anna as she walked into the room.

"Hey, sugarplum."

Anna stopped in her tracks. She had never seen her mommy looking so sad. Her eyes were puffy, and her nose was red. She looked at Liza. She wasn't crying, but she looked sad too.

"Wh-What's wrong?" she stammered.

"Oh baby," was all Melissa got out before she walked over and pulled Anna into a hug.

She didn't know what was going on, but she didn't like it, not one little bit. Her mommy had never acted like this before. She lifted her head from her mommy's shoulder and looked at her sister. "Liza, what's wrong? Why are you and mommy so sad?"

What was Liza supposed to tell her? She wasn't the adult; she shouldn't have to say anything. Her mom needed to stop crying and tell her already.

"Mom," Liza said in a slightly commanding voice. "Mom, you need to calm down and talk to Anna." When it seemed like she wouldn't listen she added, "You're scaring her. Please, just sit down and tell her what's happening."

That got Melissa's attention. She didn't want to scare her babies. She had to pull it together. She stood up, wiped her eyes, and took Anna's hand, tugging her towards the table. "Come and sit, honey. Mommy's got to talk to you about something, ok?"

Hesitantly, Anna followed and sat down.

"First, I want to tell you the same thing I told Liza. None of what's happening is your fault. Things happen in life that we don't like, but we have to stay strong for each other. Ok?"

Eying first her mom then her sister, Anna said, "Ok..."

"Daddy and I love you girls with everything we have. Nothing will ever, ever change that. Sometimes, mommies and daddies who love their babies very much, don't live together. But that doesn't change how much they love their children."

"What are you saying, Mommy?"

"Anna, daddy and I are going to be living in different houses."

"You're getting a divorce? Like Sadie's mom and dad?"

"Yes, honey. But that doesn't change how we feel about you and Liza. We both love you very much. And you will still see daddy. We will live here, and daddy will get a different house. You will get to go over every other weekend to see him. And you can call him whenever you want."

Melissa was still talking, but Anna had stopped listening. She felt like she couldn't breathe. This couldn't be happening. Her mommy and daddy could not be getting a divorce. Sadie had cried to her last year about how she never got to see her daddy ever since he moved out. And then they had moved away. She didn't want to listen anymore.

"No!" She jumped up from the table, ran to her room and slammed the door. Grabbing Emmie, she plopped down on her bed and curled up into a ball. "It's not fair. They can't do this. Mommy just told me that her and daddy are getting divorced. They can't. Mommy said that we are staying here, and daddy is leaving. But if he does, then I won't see him anymore. This can't be happening. What am I going to do, Emmie?" She continued talking and crying to Emmie until she fell asleep.

A Secret Well Kept

Chapter 14

"Honey, are you ok?" Melissa asked, walking into the girls' bedroom.

Liza didn't move from where she was laying in her bed, her back to the door. "I don't feel good."

She walked over and rubbed Liza's back. "Do you have a stomach bug? You haven't been feeling good all week. Maybe you should stay home this weekend. I'll call daddy and tell him that Anna's coming alone this weekend."

Liza sat up fast. "No. No, I'm ok. I can go. I'm fine." She jumped down off the bed. "I think you're right. It probably was the stomach bug, but it's better now." She ran to the bathroom before her mom could question her.

"Ok..." Melissa walked into the living room where Anna was waiting. "Hey, you."

"Hey. Dad texted and said he'll be here in fifteen minutes."

"Ok."

"Do you think dad would get mad if I didn't go to his house the weekend after next?"

"He probably wouldn't mind. Why? What's up?" Melissa sat down on the couch next to Anna.

"Well, you remember that boy, David, that took me to the Midwinter dance? He asked if I could go to the spring festival with him and his mom." She glanced shyly at her mom. "Think I could go?"

"Like… on a date or something? Aren't you a little young for that?"

"Mom, seriously? I'm in the sixth grade. I'm not a baby anymore. Dad got me a phone last year, so you would be able to get ahold of me anytime you need to." She gave her mom the "puppy dog" face. "Pleeease?"

Melissa laughed. "I don't care, as long as your dad says it's ok."

"Yes!" She jumped up and hugged her mom. "Thanks, mom!"

"Talk to your dad about it this weekend. It will depend on what he says."

"He'll say yes, I just know it." Hearing a horn blow outside, she gave her mom a quick kiss, hollered for Liza, and ran out the door to jump into the front seat of her dad's car.

Liza was happy to see that her dad's friend, Darlene, was staying the weekend with them. She had been over quite a few times when they were there visiting. Though not often enough for her liking; she would have preferred that Darlene was always there when they were.

"Hey, daddy, would it be ok with you if I didn't come for our next visit? Someone asked me to go somewhere with them and I really, really want to go?" Anna asked while they were eating dinner.

George looked at her sternly. "Where would you be going and with whom?"

She looked down at the table, pushing her mashed potatoes around to avoid looking at her dad. "A guy from school. He asked me if I wanted to go to the spring festival with his family."

"And do you like this boy?"

She lifted her head to meet his eyes. "He's my boyfriend, dad. We've been dating since October. I told you about him before. Remember, he's the one I went to the dance with."

"I do remember. I don't mind if you go. Darlene, your sister, and I will find something to do, I'm sure."

"Oh. George, I won't be here that weekend. I have to go out of town for work," Darlene said, touching his hand.

He smiled at her, then looked at Liza. "I guess it's just me and you then."

Liza's stomach turned. She knew what that would mean.

"So I guess this means you're growing up, doesn't it, Anna?" He gave Liza a quick wink before he turned back to Anna.

"Duh, daddy. I *am* in the sixth grade."

Liza stood suddenly. Looking around at everyone, she mumbled a quiet, "Excuse me."

She ran half blind to the restroom and slammed the door. She wouldn't cry. Not right now. She couldn't. But she didn't miss that not-so-subtle hint from her dad. Like she needed reminding. She saw it every day when she looked at her sister. She was getting older, bigger. And much harder to protect. She jumped when she heard a knock at the door.

"Liza, honey, are you ok?" Darlene asked through the door.

She took a few steadying breaths. Her mind was made up. She knew what she had to do. "Yes, my stomach is just upset. Must have been something I ate this morning. I'm ok now." She opened the door and walked back to the dining room.

"What's wrong, Liza?" Anna asked.

"Nothing, sport." Liza squeezed her sister's shoulder. Taking her seat, she looked into her dad's eyes and said, "Everything is going to be just fine."

"How do I look?" Anna asked.

"You look exactly the same as the last five times you asked me," Melissa said smiling. "You look like you are ready to have a fun time at a festival." She left to make a snack.

"Ok. What about you, Liza? Do you think I look ok?" She had on her favorite overalls with a red t-shirt underneath.

Liza abjectly replied, "Yeah, kiddo. You look great."

Anna slowly walked over to her sister. "Liza, is something wrong? You sound sad."

She took Anna in her arms and hugged her tight. "Everything is fine. I'm not sad. You're just getting so big, and I can't stop it."

Hugging her sister back, she chuckled, "You're silly, Liza. Of course I'm getting big, that's what happens when you get older."

Liza pulled her back to look into her eyes. "I know, and I love you so much. When you were born, that was the happiest moment of my life. I have loved every single day that I've had with you. I want you to know that you are the most important person in the world to me and there is nothing, *nothing*, that I wouldn't do to keep you safe."

Anna looked at her quizzically. "Um, what are you talking about? Why are you talking like it's the end of the world?"

Before she could reply, her mom walked back into the room with a plate of sliced apples and peanut butter. Casting her sister one last look, she smiled and was about to say something else when they heard a horn.

"That's odd," Melissa looked at her watch, "your father is normally never early. Maybe he has plans for you to go to dinner or something. Better not keep him waiting. I love you, honey. Have a great weekend."

Liza hugged her back long and hard before saying that she loved her. Then she walked over to Anna and pulled her into another hug. "Remember what I said," she whispered. "I love you and would do anything to protect you."

"Yeah, ok. I love you, too."

After a few more seconds, Liza let go and walked out the door. Before getting in the car, she turned back to the house and tried to push every ounce of love within her to her mom and her sister. Hopefully they would know and understand just how much she loved them.

Chapter 15

"So, how was it?" Melissa asked when Anna got back from the festival.

"It was awesome! We rode the Ferris wheel, a merry-go-round, and then I rode on a pony. His mom is funny. She kept telling me all of these little embarrassing things about him. I hardly stopped laughing all night."

"I'm glad you had a good time. Why don't you go change, then we can watch a movie or something?"

"Ok." Anna rushed to her room, still smiling about how much fun she had. While she was getting her clothes together before she showered, she thought she heard the doorbell ring, which was weird since they almost never had visitors. She didn't think too much more about it, instead remembering how it felt holding David's hand. And she couldn't wait until Liza was home so she could tell her all about her first kiss. She was still thinking about her date thirty minutes later.

"Hey, mom, do you think I could invite David over for dinner one n--" She froze on the last step when she saw her mom sitting in the middle of the living room floor, rocking and crying, while a police officer squatted next to her.

"Mom?" She waited for a response, but she wouldn't lift her head. Finally, she looked at the officer. "What happened? Why is my mom sitting on the floor crying?"

"I'm sorry, I can't answer that. Mrs. Wright, your daughter is here. She wants to know what's wrong. She needs you to talk to her."

At that, Melissa keened even louder. "Nooo! Nooo! It can't be true! It just can't be!"

Feeling more than a little frightened, Anna slowly walked closer to her mom. "Mom. Please. Tell me what's wrong. You--You're starting to scare me." When she reached her mom, she knelt down and placed a hand on her shoulder. "Mom?"

When Melissa felt her touch, she broke a little more. She grabbed Anna and pulled her into a fierce hug. "Oh, Anna, baby. I'm so sorry. I'm so sorry."

Anna hugged her back but sent a questioning look to the cop. Instead of answering she just looked at her with sympathy.

"Mom," Anna said a little more firmly. "You need to tell me what is going on."

"Liza," Melissa wailed. "Liza."

"No, Mom, I'm Anna. Tell me what's going on."

Melissa sat back just enough to look at her. She grabbed her face in both hands and held it there for a moment, then pulled her back into a hug. "I can't. I can't."

She looked again at the police officer, imploring her with her eyes. "Please, can't you just tell me what happened?"

The officer spoke to Melissa. "Ma'am?"

"I can't. I just can't."

Anna sat there a couple more minutes while her mom just cried before, finally, she had enough.

"Mom," she said pulling away, "you need to calm down and tell me what happened."

"Oh, Anna." She tried to pull her back into her arms, but Anna steadfastly held her ground. "I can't. It can't be real. I'm having a nightmare right now. This can't be real." She buried her face in her hands.

"What's not real, Mom? You can tell me. I'm right here."

"That's it. This isn't real. Just some horrible, God-awful nightmare. Liza's not dead. George isn't dead. I'll wake up and everything will be just fine."

Anna's breath froze in her lungs. "What? What did you just say?"

Melissa wiped her face and, smiling crazily, got up. "Yes. This is all a bad dream. I must have eaten something that didn't agree with my stomach, that's why I'm dreaming crazy things. Liza will be the same healthy, lovable little girl I raised, and George will still be… well, George. But they will both be alive and well in the morning." She started towards her room. "Good night, Anna. I'm sorry you were in my nightmare."

She still couldn't catch her breath. What was her mom saying? She looked again at the officer. "Please. Please tell me what she is talking about."

The officer looked back to where Melissa was walking away, then back to Anna. "I don't know how to tell you this, and I really don't think I should."

"You have to. You saw my mom. She ain't going to tell me anything. She thinks she's dreaming right now. Please, just tell me."

"There was a disturbance at your dad's house. When we got there to check it out, we found your dad and your sister."

"And?"

"They were-- they had both been shot. I'm sorry, but there was nothing we could do."

"Wh-what? How? Did you find who shot them?"

She hesitated before answering, "Well, we, uh, I think maybe you should go talk to your mom. I think she could use you right now."

Anna looked down the hall towards her mom's room. She was trying her hardest to keep it together. She had to be strong. Her mom needed her. She swallowed down her tears and said, "Yes. Ok. Um, thank you." She led them to the door.

"Are you going to be ok?"

With all the determination she could muster, she said, "Yes. Everything is going to be just fine. We'll be ok. We always are. Thank you."

She locked the door and headed to her mom's room. Once there she climbed on the bed and held her. She could feel her shaking, quietly crying. "It's ok, mom. We'll be ok. We'll get through this."

She fell asleep holding her mom and trying not to cry.

The next morning, after much coaxing, Melissa cried as she told Anna the details of what had happened.

"They said that a neighbor reported hearing gunshots. When the cops got in, they found that your dad had been shot in the living room and Liza her bedroom."

"Are they looking for who did it."

"Anna, honey. They--" She broke off, trying to calm down. "They said that they found the gun that was used. It-- It was in Liza's hand."

She tried to comprehend what her mom was saying. "But, how did she get the gun? Did someone put it there after they shot her?"

Melissa gulped and took Anna's hands. "Baby, they said that Liza did the shooting."

"But, but that would mean that-- NO!" She jumped up and started pacing the floor. "No, I can't believe that! Why would she do that?"

"I don't know. I just don't know. I know she had been acting upset the past couple weeks. But this--"

Anna stopped walking, looked at her mom and saw the agony and confusion there. She steeled herself emotionally. "I don't know why this happened, Mom. But I do know that we will make it through this. We will be here for each other now. We have to be strong."

She decided then and there that she would never forgive Liza for doing this to them. She not only took away her dad and her best friend, but she also took away her childhood. She could no longer be as carefree as she had been. She would have to act more like an adult to help her mom push past her heartache. Her days of being a kid were gone, and it was all Liza's fault.

A Secret Well Kept

Chapter 16

"Thank you for coming in so soon, Mrs. Wright," Mrs. Mauer said, opening the door and inviting her in.

Melissa walked in and sat down in the chair next to her desk. "In your note, you sounded rather urgent. Is everything ok with Anna?"

"Yes, yes. Anna is a great student. Very smart." She paused for a moment. "Do you mind if I ask you a personal question?"

She sat up a little straighter. "Ok."

"How are things going at home?"

She looked into Mrs. Mauer's eyes for a moment before answering. "Good. Better now. My family has been helping a lot."

"And how is Anna doing?"

"She's doing better. It's still hard, but better, everything considered."

"I'm glad to hear that. Her grades here at school are exceptional. She does everything I ask with no complaints."

"I've been watching her grades on progress book. I know she's doing great, so that can't be why you asked to meet." She waited patiently while Mrs. Mauer pulled a few sheets of paper from a folder on her desk.

"No, it's not. I don't want to overstep my bounds, and please, if I offend you in any way, know that is not my intent. I care very deeply for my students and want to see them succeed in every aspect of life."

"Ok…"

"It's just that, I've noticed that Anna is very…closed off. She doesn't really participate in the daily class activity. I know that what you went through is something that nobody, let alone a child, should have to go through. I was just wondering if-- has Anna ever attended counseling?"

"No. I mean, I did ask her before if she wanted to go, but she said no, and we have never really talked about it again."

"Again, please forgive me if I am overstepping, but I believe that Anna would truly benefit from it. It helps sometimes to get through things if we can talk about them."

Melissa sat up straighter. "She has me. She knows that she can talk to me about anything. I've told her that since she was young."

"Of course, I didn't mean to imply that she couldn't talk to you. It's just that, having someone who is not family to talk to about things can be a little freeing. It allows one to be able--willing to say what they are feeling deep inside."

She took a minute to really think about what Mrs. Mauer was saying. "I… I think you may be right. She's been more quiet at home as well. Thank you for suggesting it. It's… it's been hard. I was so busy when it first happened; otherwise, I may have thought more about counseling. It's been a crazy couple of years."

She handed the paper across to Melissa. "I have the names of some of the best child psychologists in the area. The ones with stars by them are ones that I have referred other children to and have had great feedback. Not to say the others aren't good, I just don't know them."

Melissa stared at the paper a moment and then back at Mrs. Mauer. Wiping a tear from her eye she whispered, "Thank you. Thank you for caring so much." She got up and offered her hand.

Mrs. Mauer also stood and gave her a warm handshake, saying, "It really is my pleasure. Like I said before, I care for the children that I teach. They are more than just students to me, they're family."

Melissa gave her one more quick smile before she let go and left.

"I don't need to go to counseling, Mom!" Anna screamed through her bedroom door. She could not believe that her mom went behind her back and set some stupid counseling meeting up without asking her. She had told her a year and a half ago that she didn't need counseling, and she still didn't. She was making it just fine. She was there for her mom when she went through the hardest times from what Liza did, she was strong for her when she had to talk to the lawyers about the insurance stuff, and was even fine when all the kids at school had found out about Liza's pregnancy. She had ignored all their stupid comments and hateful words. She had her own opinions about the whole thing. She was fine then, and she was fine now. She didn't need to talk to some stupid shrink about anything.

"Honey, some of the teachers at school are concerned. They suggested you go. They said that it might help if you were able to talk to someone."

"I talk to you. I don't need to go to a stupid shrink!"

Melissa took a slow breath in and placed her head against the door. "Anna, please. Can you go for me? It would make me happy if you did, even if just for a little while. Who knows, you might even like it."

Anna hated when her mom said stuff like that. She knew that she would do anything for her when she asked like that. She would do whatever her mom wanted if it meant keeping her happy. They've both had so much sadness in their lives that she didn't want to add to it.

"Fine. I'll go. But if I don't like it, I want to be allowed to stop."

"You'll give it at least 3 months, going every Saturday, before you quit?"

Anna gritted her teeth and took a deep breath. "Okay. But after that, you can't get upset if I decide I don't want to go anymore, right?"

"Deal. Now, come out and let's go to the Chinese buffet by the mall for dinner."

Oh yeah, her mom knew how to manipulate her. She knew that was her favorite place to eat.

Chapter 17

"How was your week, Anna?" Dr. Nancy Scott asked after settling down in one of the matching red, oversized recliners in her office.

"It was good. Danny finally asked me out."

"He did? And you said…"

"I told him yes, of course." Anna said laughing. She and Dr. Scott had grown close over the past couple of years. She could still remember arguing with her mom about going to counseling, but that was before she met Dr. Scott. She had expected some old lady who she wouldn't like, let alone be able to talk to. Dr. Scott was *not* old, and she was very pretty and down to Earth. Anna liked her a lot and had grown to trust her.

"He asked last week. As soon as I left here, he called and we went to the movies that night. We also hung out every single day, but," Anna grew more quiet and serious, "he always wants me to go to his house."

"And you don't want to?"

"It's not that I don't want to, it's just, I don't know. His dad kinda gives me the heeby jeebies."

Dr. Scott sat up a little straighter. This was the first time in all of their talks that she felt like Anna was starting to talk about something more than the everyday stuff.

"What does he do that gives you the 'heeby jeebies'?" she asked with a reassuring smile and wink.

She squirmed a little before answering, "I don't know. He don't really *do* anything. He's a nice person, just very huggy. It just makes me feel a little uncomfortable."

"Does he hug *you*?" She asked with a little incredulity.

"Right!? You think it's a little weird, too! I mean, like, I don't like any man hugging me, let alone someone I just met."

"Yes, *totally* weird. What do you do when he tries to hug you? Punch him in the stomach and say, 'Yo, back it up, weirdo.'"

Anna laughed, "Oh my gosh, no. But that would be funny."

Dr. Scott laughed a little longer. She didn't want to push, but she also didn't want to let this opportunity get away. Still smiling she said, "Can I ask you a question?"

"Don't you always?" She chuckled.

"Touché. Ok, so you said you don't like any man hugging you?"

Anna didn't answer right away. Instead, she stared and debated within herself. She was quiet for almost two full minutes before she replied, "No. I don't."

"Why do you think that is?"

"I don't *think* I know why it is, I *know* why."

Instead of asking why, Dr. Scott leaned back on her oversized, plush chair and just waited patiently for her to continue.

"I don't trust men." After a brief pause, she continued, "Can I tell you something? A secret."

"Anna, you know that you can tell me anything."

She squirmed in the recliner that she was sitting in. Sliding off her Crocs, she slowly pulled her legs up to her chest. Wrapping her arms around them, she continued, "It's something that I never told anyone."

She sat forward in her chair and took Anna's hands. "You can tell me absolutely anything."

"I don't trust men... because they do stuff that I don't like."

"What do they do?"

"They touch me... and other stuff."

She did her best to keep her voice light and soft. "What do you mean they touch you?"

"Like, in places that they're not supposed to be touching."

"When?" She asked gently. "When did this happen?"

"When I was younger."

"How old?"

Anna looked up and searched her eyes. "Which time?"

Dr. Scott froze in stunned disbelief. Looking passionately at Anna, she asked, "How many times has this happened?"

"Three." She had never talked to anyone about this before, unless you count her old doll, Emmie. She quickly wiped at the tear that had escaped before saying, "Look, I really don't want to talk about it. It happened when I was a kid. There is no reason to start talking about it now, it won't change anything."

Chapter 18

After staring at her for a few seconds, Dr. Scott finally asked, "Can I tell you a story?"

Shocked that she was going to let it go so easily, Anna nodded.

Dr. Scott set down her pen and notebook and folded her hands together, resting her elbows on her knees. "This is a story that I don't really like to talk about, but in this case, I think I should. When I was fourteen, I played volleyball for the girl's high school varsity team. I was the youngest girl on the team, but I was good, really good. We would play in all the local tournaments, state tournaments, and even had some overnight tournaments that were out of state. The coach said I was the best player he had ever coached, especially for how young I was. I would stay after practice quite often to get extra practice in. I was extremely competitive and had to be the best." She gave Anna a wink and a smile. "My coach was always very helpful and supportive of me trying to better my game. He would give me advise, adjust my stance, teach me better techniques. It wasn't unusual for him to touch me in order to make sure I was using the correct form. I never really thought much about his closeness, I was that focused on getting better. At the end of the school year, he talked to me about a volleyball summer camp. I didn't think my parents would let me go, but he talked them into it by saying that it would help me get more scholarships for college and assuring them that he would watch out for me since he was one of the counselors. It was a five-day camp. I was super excited since I had never been to an overnight camp like that before. I think I had everything packed before school even got out." Her smile slowly faded as she continued, "But nothing could have prepared me for what happened when I got there. The camp was crazy nice. I shared a cabin with five other girls. Of course, they were all older than me, but we got along well so nobody really cared. The first night there they were all talking about how Chris, my coach, was the cutest coach they had ever seen. They made all kinds of little comments that I would not want to repeat, but it was all in good fun. I didn't join in on their commenting because to me he was just coach. I didn't pay attention to if he was cute or not. I just wanted to play volleyball. It was my obsession, and my escape. My parents argued a lot. I would always go outside and practice so I didn't have to hear it. Anyway, every day we would have one on one time with our counselors to learn ways that would better our individual game. My counselor, of course, was Chris. During my first day of one-on-one time, he was helping me with my ready stance. He was saying that I needed to get lower in my squat. While he was telling me this, he put his hands on my hips, nudging me lower. I was so focused on my squat that I didn't notice that his hands had traveled to my butt. It was the first time he had ever touched me like that. He stopped there though. He moved his hands back to my hips and then went on with the rest of practice like nothing had happened. That night as I laid on my bed, I convinced myself that what I thought had happened didn't really happen. It couldn't have. This was Chris. He was my coach. I trusted him. It was all the talk the older girls were doing that was making my imagination run wild.

"The next day at my one-on-one time, I was slightly hesitant to go in the gym room, but I really wanted to be a professional volleyball player, so I shrugged it off and went on in. That day we worked on arm position while hitting the ball. I told him that I was already good at that, but he insisted that I needed to 'always be open to learning and bettering myself.' I shrugged and said ok. He told me to show him my stance for bumping the ball, so I did. As I stood there holding my position, he walked around making small adjustments. Then he stood behind me and put his arms around me, stretching them out to the position mine were in. As he was whispering about the importance of keeping my arms straight, he traced his hands up my arms on the underside until he was rubbing his hands against my chest. I froze. I think I kind of "locked-up" mentally and physically. I couldn't believe that my coach was touching me like that. Just like the last time though, he only did it for a couple seconds, then pretended that nothing happened and continued with the lesson. I was so confused. Surely that didn't just happen. I don't think I even remember the rest of that class; I was so shaken up. Right before I walked out at the end, he said that since the next day was the last class before we went home, he had something extra special planned. Something that would take me to a whole other level. I assumed he was talking about volleyball, but honestly, I didn't really think too much about it. My mind was still spinning over what had happened.

"I spent that night curled up on my bed, replaying every moment that I had ever spent with him. Trying to see if there was ever a time that something like that had happened before, but I couldn't think of one. He was always very helpful and nice, but he never had done that before. I wondered if I should tell someone or not, but I think I may have been in denial. I didn't want to believe that this guy that I looked up to so much would do such a thing. By the next day, I had talked myself into believing that it was all in my head, that nothing really happened. When it was time for one-on-one, I won't lie and say that I wasn't a little nervous. But I went, if only to prove to myself that it wasn't real. He was waiting by the weight room when I got there. When I questioned him on it, he said that we were mixing it up a little and working on our strength training. I think I was a little relieved because I thought that it meant he wouldn't be right up on me like in the gym. But I was wrong." She took a deep breath before continuing, "He took my hand once we got inside. Asked me to come to the office for a minute before we started. Said he wanted to show me some college scholarship stuff. When we got there, he pushed me onto the couch and raped me."

Anna sat up quickly and inhaled sharply.

"I tried to fight him, but he was too strong. Afterwards, while I laid there crying, he told me that if I ever told anyone what happened, he would make sure I never played volleyball again.

Besides, he had said, nobody would believe me anyway."

"Did you ever tell?"

She gave her a sad smile. "I didn't right away. I think I was afraid. Like maybe people would say it was my fault or something. My parents picked me up that Friday after camp. By Sunday they knew something was wrong. As much as they argued with each other, they were always attentive to me. They questioned me about why I seemed so down. I beat around the bush for about fifteen minutes before, through a sea of tears, I finally told them what happened."

"What did they do? Did they get mad at you?"

She looked quizzically at Anna for a second while deciding on the best answer. She knew that this question was about more than her story. "No. How could they be mad at something that was done to me? Something that was, by no means, my fault. They knew that what he did was wrong and that something had to be done."

There was a moment's silence before Anna quietly asked, "What did they do?"

"Well, they told the police and took me to see a special doctor that helps girls who have been raped. Chris was arrested and sentenced to ten years in prison. My parents had me talk to a counselor about what happened. It helped a lot to be able to talk about all of the fears that I had after that. In fact, I think what happened to me is the main reason I wanted to become a counselor. Someone was there to help me when I needed it, so I wanted to be there to help others, in any way possible. Whether it be talking about boys," she gave a playful wink, "about grades, about parents. Absolutely anything."

She looked intently at Anna. "I know that talking about things that have happened, especially *those* kinds of things, is extremely difficult. I know that it hurts and that it's scary. But I also know that it is freeing." Here she stopped and just waited.

Finally, Anna looked down at her lap and said, "Ok, I'll tell you what happened. But after this, I never want to talk about it again, ok?"

Lifting her eyes to meet Dr. Scott's she saw that her hand was held out in front of her. After the briefest moment, she took her hand and shook it.

"Deal."

A Secret Well Kept

Chapter 19

Taking a deep breath, Anna told her about the first two times she was "touched."

When it seemed like she was done talking, Dr. Scott said, "I cannot tell you how sorry I am that those men took advantage of you like that." She pulled her in for a small but meaningful hug. Settling back against the chair again she asked, "Didn't you say there were three instances? What happened the third time?"

This was the hardest one to tell. Anna had never told anybody about this one, not even Emmie, who had known everything that happened to her. But Dr. Scott had said that they could talk about it this one time, and that it would help her heal on the inside. She sure hoped so, because she hated always being afraid.

"It was the summer after I turned seven. We were on our annual camping trip, when my Uncle Robert showed up. Dad had invited him, said he 'needed to be around family.' I was a little upset since it was supposed to only be us, but I wasn't too mad. I liked my uncle. He was my dad's younger brother, and he always gave me candy. Anyway, that night dad got a call from his office. Mom told us that they had to leave to take care of something and that Uncle Robert would watch us and bring us home on Sunday. I was mad, but again, not too mad, Uncle Robert was fun. That night me and Liza was watching a movie in the living room, and she fell asleep. I was laying on the couch still watching it when Robert walked through from his bedroom to the kitchen. He came over, sat beside me and watched a little bit of the movie before asking me if I wanted to come to his room. He said he wanted to show me something really neat out his window. So I got up and went to his room. I walked over to the window and looked out, but he didn't follow. Instead, he got in his bed and laid under the covers. When I saw that he was in bed, I said that I thought he wanted to show me something neat. He said that he did and to come lay down with him for a little while first. He said we had to lay there to really see it. Like a dummy, I believed him and laid down next to him. I kept looking out the window waiting to see what was there when he asked me if I liked to play with marbles." Anna paused to take a shaky breath. She lowered her voice to a whisper and continued, "When I said yes, he...he took my hand and told me that I could play with his marbles. Then he put my hand on his private area. I didn't want to touch him, but he made my fingers move around. I almost cried with relief when he let me stop and I could move my hand away. But he wasn't done." Anna swiped at a tear that had escaped her eye. "He asked me if I liked lollipops, and stupidly I said that I did. He asked if I liked honey, and again, I answered yes. Then he had me-- He made me--" Anna tried to finish the sentence, but tears were streaming down her face which was red with shame.

Dr. Scott leaned forward and touched her shoulder and whispered, "It's ok, Anna. You don't need to finish that sentence. I think I know what came next. That is a terrible, terrible thing that happened."

Anna sniffed and wiped her eyes before continuing, "But that's not the end of it." She took a shuddering breath to try to calm herself. "When he walked me back to the living room, he knelt down by the couch and told me that he was sorry. I didn't know what else to say, so I said ok. The next morning it was like he never did anything. He was all smiling and joking around like always. He took us hiking and swimming. I didn't want Liza to know what had happened, so I pretended that nothing did. But that night, we were watching a movie again. This time he watched it with us. Me and Liza was sitting on the floor when I complained that my butt was hurting from it. I started to go sit in the chair, but Uncle Robert said that I could lay down on the couch with him. He said it would be more comfortable. Again, I didn't want Liza to know anything was wrong, so I did. He pulled back the blanket and snuggled me up really close to him. When he wriggled me around to get me closer, my nightgown slid up. All I had under it was my panties. It wasn't too long before Liza fell asleep. I thought Robert fell asleep too, so I started to get up and move away. But he wasn't asleep. Right as I started to stand up, he reached out and grabbed my wrist. He told me to lay back down so that I didn't wake Liza up. I really didn't want to... but I did. I tried to keep my nighty down when I laid back down, but he just pushed it back up. I started crying quietly; I was so afraid. I laid there for a while wide awake. Just when I thought it was going to be ok, that he fell asleep, I felt his hands start moving. He-- He pulled my panties open and-- Well, I found out that he was not wearing his underwear. Then he-- He put his private area by mine. I wanted to scream. I wanted to tell him to stop, but I was too afraid to move. After laying like that for a while longer, I felt him start to move around. I was so afraid of what he was going to do next, but he just kissed my head and got up. I almost passed out with relief; I was so happy he was leaving. He leaned down before he walked out and whispered that he was sorry again."

124

Chapter 20

Dr. Scott was surprised to find that she, too, had tears streaming down her face. She got up and got them both a tissue from her desk. "What happened when you told your mom and dad?"

Anna sat straight up. "I didn't tell them. I told you that I never told anyone about what happened."

"Why didn't you tell them?"

"The first two people moved away, so I don't have to worry about them anymore. And Uncle Robert said he was sorry; I had to forgive him. So I don't need to tell them about him, either. Besides, last I heard he was in jail already."

"Anna, honey, you have to tell your mom. Those men need to be punished for what they did."

She stood, all her pain turning into anger. "No. I don't want her to know. We've already gone through enough crap, I don't want to add to it."

"I know that you don't want to tell her. I understand, truly. But this is not something that we can keep from her."

Anna walked over to the window and looked out. "No. I won't tell her. I can't."

"I will be right here with you if you want, but you have to tell her."

"No, I don't."

Dr. Scott took a long, deep breath. She didn't like what she was about to do, but she had no choice in the matter. She waited for Anna to turn around and looked at her, then she said, "You're right, you don't."

Anna's shoulders sagged with relief as she turned back towards the window. She never wanted to tell her mom about what happened. She only told Dr. Scott because she had told her story. And besides, she said it would help her. Telling her mom would most definitely not help. Her mom might get mad at her and then she would have nobody left.

"But I do."

She whirled so fast she almost fell. "What!? What do you mean you do? You can't tell her. You said when we first met that whatever I said in this room stayed in this room?"

She sighed. "I did, but I have to tell this."

"No, you don't. Ain't there a rule or something that says you can't since I'm your patient or whatever?"

"There is, but there is also a rule that says if a child is being hurt, I must, by law, report it."

She crossed over to the chair and sat down. She looked her in the eyes and earnestly said, "But I'm not being hurt. It all happened in the past."

"That is true, but since you are still a minor, it has to be reported."

Anna stared a moment longer. "Please, I am begging you. Don't tell my mom. I haven't seen my uncle since my dad died. Like I said, he's in jail. My mom don't need any more stress than she already has. Please, just don't."

Dr. Scott wiped at the tears that were forming in her eyes. "Anna, I'm sorry. I really am. But this is not something that can be kept a secret, especially from your mom. I know it's hard and that you're afraid, but it will help you in the long run."

"No, it won't. It will only make things harder at home. You don't understand. My mom needs me to be strong for her. If you tell her, it will make me look weak."

Dr. Scott reached over and gently placed her hands on Anna's and gave it a gentle squeeze. "I have to tell her, Anna."

Anna jerked her hands away. "I won't forgive you if you do."

Dr. Scott looked down at her now empty hands for a moment before meeting Anna's eyes once more. "I'm sorry you feel that way, but I can't not tell your mom. Not only is it the law, but it's also the right thing to do."

Anna stood up and walked to the door, looking back one last time before slamming the door behind her and rushing out to her mom's car.

Chapter 21

"Anna," Melissa said, putting a hand to her chest. "You scared me." She looked at the time on her phone. "It's only 11:15. Did you finish early today?"

She didn't look at her mom. She couldn't look at her. "Yes, we're done. Can we go home, please?"

Melissa stared at her for a second longer before nodding and putting the car in drive.

Anna was silent on the drive home. As soon as they pulled up to the house, Anna said that she didn't feel good and was going to lay down. She jumped out of the car and ran straight for her bedroom. Closing the door, she plopped down on her bed. She wouldn't cry over this. She had to be strong. She *would* be strong.

That Monday, Anna was hopeful that since Dr. Scott hadn't talked to her mom yet, she had changed her mind. That she realized she couldn't tell Anna's secret. She figured that if she hadn't called yet, then she wasn't going to at all. So when she walked in the door after school and saw her Aunt Megan and her mom sitting on the couch crying, she was hit with the dread that she had been suppressing all weekend. She wished she could just walk back out the door and pretend she didn't see them, but before she could, her mom jumped up and rushed to her with outstretched arms.

"Oh, Anna!"

"Mom, what--" was all she got out before she was enveloped in a hug so tight she could barely breathe. The next thing she knew her Aunt Meg was hugging her, too.

She let them hug her a few seconds more before extricating herself. Deciding to play dumb she asked, "What's wrong with you guys?"

Melissa took her hand, pulled her towards the couch and sat her down. "Anna, honey, we know."

Keeping up with her charade she asked, "Know what?" She looked back and forth between the two of them.

It was her Aunt Meg who answered. "Dr. Scott called your mom this morning. Said that she needed to see her as soon as possible. I was here visiting, so I went with her. When she came out of the office, she was so upset. I couldn't get her to stop crying long enough to tell me what was wrong until we got back home." Her aunt reached out and grabbed one of Anna's hands.

"She told me that Dr. Scott told her what those animals did to you."

Anna wanted to run and hide. She wished she had never told Dr. Scott what happened. She could have dealt with it on her own, but no, she had to go and tell the doctor who just had to tell her mom. Then, of course, her mom told her sister. She really hoped that nobody else would find out. She didn't need anyone else to know how ashamed she was.

"Why didn't you tell me?" Melissa asked, drawing Anna's attention back to her.

"Because." What was she supposed to say? Because she was trying to protect her? That she knew how hard things were with her and her dad, so she didn't want to add anything else to it? No. She couldn't say any of that. Her mom had always tried to hide any argument that she had with her dad. She never let them see when she was hurting, so neither did Anna.

"Because why?" Searching her daughter's eyes, she continued, "Why wouldn't you tell me? I've always said that you can tell me anything. You told me about all of your little crushes, your dreams, your nightmares. Why didn't you tell me this?"

"Because it was in the past. They moved away so I never had to see them again. I didn't think it was important to tell you afterwards. I just put it behind me."

Melissa took Anna in her arms again. "Anna," she said as she squeezed her to her chest, "you are important. Everything that happens to you is important to me. Especially something like this."

Just as she was about to reply, Anna jumped when the front door slammed open, and her uncle came rushing in.

"I'll kill them!"

Her Uncle Frank was like that, always so dramatic. She knew he meant well, but sometimes he could be a little intense.

"Hi, Uncle Frank." she muffled through his chest as he engulfed her and Melissa in his arms.

He pulled them back and looked into Anna's eyes. "Are you ok? Tell me where they are, and I will hunt them down and kill them."

"It's ok. Really. It's done and over with. I can't change it, nobody can."

"Maybe not, but I can dismember the SOB that hurt my family!"

Anna pulled herself away from them all. She really just wanted to pretend this whole thing never happened.

"Please, can we not talk about this? It's not helping, it's just making it worse," she pleaded with them.

Her mom, aunt, and uncle had a silent conversation with their eyes. Finally, her mom had agreed to not talk about it, for now.

"Thank you. If it's ok, I'm going to head to bed."

Without giving any hugs, she walked to her room. As she closed the door, she could hear her uncle start talking again. She paused to listen.

"...unacceptable. If I ever find them, I *will* kill them. Nobody hurts my family and lives to tell about it."

She'd heard enough. She closed the door and laid down on her bed. She just wanted to go to sleep and pretend her family wasn't in the other room talking about the stuff she desperately wanted to put behind her. She never wanted to think about it, let alone anyone find out. She let out a deep sigh, turned over to her side and fell into a restless sleep.

The next morning, Anna was relieved to find that her aunt and uncle weren't there. It was just her mom sitting at the dining room table behind a steaming cup of coffee. She almost stopped. She was normally the one who woke up early to make coffee for her mom, so to see her already up with a cup gave Anna a moment's pause. Instead, she pasted a smile on her face and walked past her mom to the kitchen.

"I'm making me an egg for breakfast. Do you want one?" She asked as she pulled out a skillet from under the stove. She waited a beat to see if there would be a reply. When there wasn't, she knew her mom wasn't going to put this behind her so easily.

After making an egg and toast, she poured herself some apple juice and walked back into the dining room. She sat down and instead of eating right away, she just stared at her mom. If she wanted to have it out, then so be it. Anna had planned exactly what she would say while she was cooking. Her mom was just going to have to sit there and take what she was saying. She didn't want to rehash what happened. She refused to. If she was letting it go, then her mom would have to, too.

When Melissa finally looked up, she was surprised to see Anna sitting there. She must have been completely consumed in her thoughts. She didn't hear Anna wake up, let alone go into the kitchen and make food. She knew why her mind wasn't there, of course. She was still beating herself up mentally for what she had allowed to happen to her baby. She didn't think she got even a minute of sleep last night. After her brother and sister left, she just sat on the couch crying quietly so as not to wake Anna up.

"Mom."

She must have zoned off again. "I'm sorry, honey. Did you say something?"

Anna stared at her mom for a moment, trying to judge if she was just trying to play coy. "Mom, I know you want to talk more about everything, but I don't. I really am ok. I just want to move on with my life, just like we did when Liza killed dad."

Melissa sucked in her breath. They never talked about that. Not that she didn't want to. But Anna never seemed to want to discuss it when she tried to bring it up. But now, to hear her put it so brutally. "Anna--"

She held up her hand to stop her mom. "Look, I get it. You were surprised. It was a shock. But it's not for me. Way back when it happened, yes it was a shock. But now... Mom, I've moved on from it. What good is talking about it going to do?"

"But--"

Forcefully setting her fork on the table, Anna firmly said, "No." She hated talking to her mom like a child, but sometimes she felt like she was the adult. She had since her dad died. She had to be the strong one then and she had to be now. Her mom obviously couldn't handle this. Changing her tone to that of one placating a child, she continued, "Look, mom, I know you don't understand that I never told you about what happened. But, I mean, it was so long ago that now there really is no need to discuss it." She pulled out her trump card. "Besides, I think talking about it might make it harder for me." She knew that her mom would do anything to prevent her from being hurt.

Melissa reached out and took Anna's hand. "Sweetie, maybe we should try. Dr. Scott said that I needed to talk to you about it. That talking would be the best th--"

"Mom. I talked to her already. I know what will and will not hurt me. I told her that I was over it. I told her that we didn't need to tell you or anyone else. But she didn't listen."

"I'm glad she told me. I needed to know."

"But don't you see? I don't need to talk about it anymore. Dragging up all that stuff would not be good for me." She squeezed her hand and looked deep into her eyes. "Please,

Mom. Can you just do this for me? I would rather we put this behind us and focus on what's important...college." When Melissa's eyes sparked with a hint of excitement, Anna smiled to herself. She knew just what to say to make her mom happy.

"So, you decided that you *are* going to go?"

"Yes. But I need you to focus on *that* with me, not the past. Deal?" She held out her hand.

She could see the hesitation in her mom's eyes. Finally, Melissa stuck out her hand and shook hers. "Deal."

"Good." She picked up her egg sandwich and took a big bite. Around the food she asked, "So, want to go shopping Saturday? I could really use a new pair of jeans. Plus, I want to put some applications in. Star told me that there are a couple places in the mall that hires fifteen-year-olds."

"Um...You have an appointment with Dr. Scott Saturday. You know that."

"Mom, I've been going for two years already. I don't think I need to go anymore."

"But, Anna, with everything that I just found out, I would think you should go more and maybe talk through things."

She stood and, picking up her plate, said, "Mom, I told you that I didn't want to talk about the past. I didn't mean that I didn't want to talk about it just to you. I don't want to talk about it period. So going back to Dr. Scott now would be pointless."

When it looked like Melissa was going to argue the point, Anna said, "Look, remember when I first started going? You said that I only had to go for a couple months, then I could stop if I wanted to. Well, it's been way longer than that and I don't want to go anymore."

"But maybe you should."

"Or I shouldn't. Please, mom."

After a few seconds of staring, Melissa relented and said that if Anna really didn't feel like she needed or wanted to go, then she wouldn't make her.

"Thank you." She gave her mom a kiss on the cheek as she passed to clean her dishes. She was relieved that she didn't have to argue about going. She would have won because she was not going back to see that back-stabbing, two-faced traitor. But it was ok, she learned that she couldn't trust people with her secrets. She would just keep them to herself like she had up until that point.

Chapter 22

"Mom, it's not that big of a deal," Anna said, sliding the last of her books into the new book bag her aunt had bought after she declared to those at her graduation party that she was starting her college classes that fall.

"Of course it is," Melissa replied while taking yet another picture. "It's not every day my little girl starts her first day of college." *Snap.* "Do you know" *Snap* "how absolutely proud" *Snap* "I am of you?" *Snap.*

Anna held her hand out in front of her. "Ok, ok," she laughed. She leaned in and gave her mom a quick kiss on the cheek. "I've got to go, or I'll be late."

"Ok," she said pulling her in for a hug. She didn't want to let go but knew that she had to. Her daughter had grown up so fast. She wished that she could go back in time and keep both of her daughters young and free from pain. After another second, she let her go. "But one more before you leave."

Before she could protest, her mom brought the camera up and snapped another picture. She just laughed as she walked out the door. "Bye! Love you!" she called over her shoulder as she rushed down the walkway.

On her way to school she thought back to how her mom reacted when she told her that she was going to major in Psychology.

"Psychology?" Melissa asked, wrinkling her nose. "You aren't going into the arts?"

"No," Anna stated.

"But... you used to say you wanted to go to art school. You love drawing and painting."

"I do."

"Then...why aren't you going to go to an arts school?"

"I want to be a Psychologist."

"Why?" She couldn't understand why she would give up on her love for all things art.

"I know I stopped seeing Dr. Scott, but I am glad that I went there. It made me see the need for more people like her." She paused a moment and looked intently in her mom's eyes. "With everything that's happened to us these past years, we made it through. I want to be there to help others who are going through stuff of their own."

Melissa couldn't argue with that kind of logic. Her daughter had always been the kind of girl who would give her right hand if someone needed it. She smiled and pulled her into a long hug. "I am so proud of the young woman you've become."

Anna was so deep in thought after her first class that she didn't notice the boy sitting underneath the tree until she tripped over his outstretched legs.

"Oof!" she exclaimed as her knee slammed into the ground. Luckily it was grass so her knee wasn't hurt. Unfortunately, she couldn't say the same about her pride.

"Are you ok?" A hand reached out to pick up the book she had been carrying.

She didn't look at him as she got up and dusted the grass from her jeans. "I'm ok and I'm sorry. I wasn't paying attention to where I was walking."

"It's ok." He stood up with her. "Psychology, huh?"

She lifted her eyes quickly to his. "How did you--" she stopped when she saw her book in his hand. "Oh." She dropped her eyes again and reached out to take her book. "Yeah. Well, thank you. And again, I'm sorry for falling fo--over you." What was wrong with her? It was like she had never talked to a cute boy before. She grabbed the book and turned quickly to walk away.

"Hey, wait up!" he said, trotting to catch up. "What's the hurry?"

"What? Nothing I--" she sighed. "I-- I just have to get to my next class." Even though she still had thirty minutes before class started. She couldn't stay there and get even more embarrassed.

"Where are you headed?"

She looked at her schedule before replying, "Biology."

"Professor Reid?"

Looking again she answered, "Yes." Slowing her steps and daring to meet his gaze she asked, "Do you know him?"

"I had him last year. He's tough, but he's also a great teacher. As long as you put forth the effort, he will do everything he can to help you succeed."

"Good to know."

"I'm Alex."

She hesitated for just a moment. "Anna."

"So, first year, huh?"

She stopped abruptly. "How do you know that?"

He gave a little chuckle. "Most first years take biology."

"Oh. How about you?"

"Yep."

She wrinkled her nose in confusion. "Yes, you did too? Or yes, you are a first-year student?"

"Yes, I did too. I'm in my third year."

"What's your major?"

"Criminal Justice."

"Really?" She eyed his shoulder length hair, torn jeans, and flip flops. She would have pictured a Criminal Justice major dressed a lot neater. Maybe nice slacks, polo shirt, clean cut hair.

He looked down at himself then back at her with a little mischief in his eyes. "What? You can't tell?"

"No, I--. That's not what I--"

"Relax, I'm just giving you a hard time. I know I don't look like the other CJ majors here. I like to be my own person, though. You know?"

"Oh, um, yeah. I-- I know what you mean."

She really didn't though. For as long as she could remember she had always had to be someone else. From the time her dad died, she was no longer able to be her own, she was a rock. She had to make sure she was always strong for her mom. For weeks after that horrible incident, she had been afraid her mom would not recover. She refused to eat, barely drank, never left the house. Anna learned very fast how to check the bank account, pay the bills, buy the groceries.

She was relieved when she came across that letter in her mom's drawer while putting her clothes away. It had been a letter from her Aunt Megan. She couldn't remember her mom ever talking about her, but the letter made it clear that her mom could call on her anytime she needed her. She didn't like how it had talked about her dad, but that wasn't important. What was important was that there was someone out there who could come help. She knew that she had missed too much school already so when this "Aunt Megan" showed up after Anna called, it was such a relief that she nearly cried. But she didn't, she had to be strong. Before all that, she still hadn't been her own. Before that she had to be a wall; a wall so long and tall that no secrets could get past. Those men made her into that. The way they all—No. She would not think about that stuff. She said she was letting it go, so she was. She hadn't realized that she had been quiet for so long until she heard Alex talking to her.

"Hello?" He waved his hand a little in front of her face. "Are you still in there?"

She pulled back slightly. "What? Yes, of course. I'm sorry. What were you saying?"

"Are you ok? You looked like you went somewhere else for a minute there."

"Yeah, I'm fine. Sorry about that. I just got lost in some memories."

"Must have been some bad ones from the look you had on your face."

She stared at him. "They were, but I'd rather not talk about them." She glanced at the time on her phone. "Oh, I'd better hurry." She turned to walk away from him. "I only have twenty minutes to get across campus and then try to figure out where my class is."

"Wait up. I'll show you where it is," he said jogging up to her.

"You don't have to."

"I want to."

"I really don't want you to have to go out of your way. I'm sure I can find it."

He placed a hand gently on her shoulder as they continued to walk. "Really, I want to. And it's not too far out of the way."

She tensed up slightly when he touched her. She didn't hear what he said because she was too busy repeating her mantra in her head. *It doesn't mean anything. It doesn't mean anything. It's just a friendly gesture. It doesn't mean anything.* Yes, she had put the past behind her, but sometimes it liked to pop up. She just had to learn how to put it back where it belonged, behind her. Still, she was relieved when he removed his hand after only a second.

"Ok, if you're sure." He was cute, funny and confident. Now she could add nice to his repertoire.

Chapter 23

"So, what do you think?" Alex asked getting up from the sofa to get another soda.

"I don't know."

"Come on, Anna. You'll love it. Everyone at my church is awesome. They really care about people, and not just the ones that look and think like them. They are the most accepting group of people I've ever met."

"Still. I mean, I think it's great that you have your faith, but I don't know that I could be like that."

"What do you mean?" he asked settling next to her again.

"I don't know. You just make believing look so easy." They had been dating for almost five months and she had never seen him so much as hesitate in his belief that God was with him. Not even last month when he was in a car accident and his car got totaled by someone running a stop sign. Instead of getting angry, he just left the hospital saying that he was glad God had His hand on him and that he hoped the other person was ok. She didn't think she would have acted so calm.

"Faith isn't always easy. Even when I don't see a way out, I have faith that God will always make one. Maybe not in the way I would like, but I believe that His ways are greater than mine, and that He will make everything work together for my good." He let her think on what he had said for a minute. "Please come with me?" He took her hand and gave it a gentle squeeze. "If you don't like it, I will never ask you to come again." He used his other hand to mark an "X" over his heart. "Cross my heart."

She stared at their intertwined hands. She wanted to go, but she wasn't completely sure. She had tried but couldn't completely let go of the anger over everything she has been through. She didn't let it show, but it was there just under the surface.

He could tell that she was really considering it. He hadn't invited her before. He wanted to but felt that it would be best if they knew each other better. Now, he was sure he loved her and wanted to share the best kind of Love with her. "It would mean a lot to me. I'm singing a special today and would love to have you supporting me out there."

She gave him a gentle punch on the arm. "That was a low blow. You know I would do anything to support you. You just had to throw that in there, didn't you?" She smiled so he knew she wasn't upset.

"Yep." He smiled back. "Did it work?"

They stared at each other for a few more seconds before she caved. "Yes," she chuckled.

He leaned in to steal a kiss. She wrapped her arms around his neck and stretched it out into a longer, deeper kiss.

"Thank you. It really does mean a lot to me," he said, breaking the kiss and pulling her into a hug.

She felt so safe in his arms, so protected. She never wanted him to let go. "You're welcome." She squeezed him a little harder.

Anna sat in total amazement as the pastor spoke about the very thing she and Alex had talked about.

"Did you tell him what I said to you about your faith looking so easy?" she whispered in his ear.

"No," he whispered back. "Sometimes God just works like that. It's called confirmation of the Spirit."

She gave him a confused look.

"Meaning that what I said to you and what the pastor is saying both came from God. He used me to say it first, now He's using the pastor to confirm it."

"Oh." She focused her attention back on the pastor.

"…like He said in Matthew 17:20. 'If you have the faith of a mustard seed, you can say to this mountain, "Move," and it will move. Nothing will be impossible for you.' Does this mean that a physical mountain will move if you command it to in Jesus name? Maybe. But what this passage says to me is that if I am facing any kind of spiritual mountain in my life, if I have the faith, I can command that mountain to move. What I find even more awesome than that is that the same God that commanded the wind and waves to be still is the same God that walks with me every single second of my life. He never leaves us nor forsakes us. He may not calm every storm in my life, but He will calm me enough to remember that nothing is ever too big for my God. 'But pastor, you don't understand. You don't know what storms I've had to face.' You're right, I don't. But I do know that He will see you through anything that you have to face in this life. If you give it to Him, He will give you a way. In Matthew 7:7 it says that all we need to do is ask. 'Keep on asking, and you will receive what you ask for. Keep on seeking, and you will find. Keep on knocking, and the door will be opened to you.' I like this version. 'Keep on knocking.' Don't give up. Don't lose faith. Does this mean you will get everything you ask for? No. God, in His infinite wisdom, knows what is best for us. 'But pastor, I have been asking for so long. God isn't answering.' Or is He. Sometimes God's answer isn't the same as what we are hoping for. Maybe we prayed for someone to not be sick anymore, but they weren't healed. Do we give up on God? No. We need to keep faith that He has a perfect plan for each of us. 'But pastor, if you knew everything that I've been through you would understand that I just can't have that kind of faith.' To that I say to think about everything that Christ went through. God willingly stepped down off His throne to become flesh, just like you and me. He faced the same temptations as every other human being. He went through some *stuff*. He was betrayed by one of His closest friends. He was abused and mistreated by the very people He came to save. But do you know what His response was? 'Father, forgive them.' Forgive them. He wasn't hanging on the cross angry at the men who put Him there. He pitied them. He asked for them to be forgiven. He set the very example of love that He wants us to have. Matthew 6:14 says, 'For if you forgive other people when they sin against you, your heavenly Father will also forgive you.' Forgive for your own salvation. It's not easy, but it is worth a heavenly reward.

"One more thing before I close; when we are mistreated, we need to take a moment and remember who our real enemy is. It isn't that person who did wrong to us, it's the spirit leading that person's actions. Ephesians 6:12 says, 'For we wrestle not against flesh and blood, but against principalities, against powers, against the rulers of the darkness of this world, against spiritual wickedness in high places.' Yes, that person may have hurt you, but your real battle is with the devil. When you feel the urge to hate the person that did you wrong, start praying for them and praising God and watch the miracles He will do in and through you."

Anna sat there stunned. It felt like everything he was saying was directed straight to her. She looked around as the music played, wondering if everyone else knew that he was preaching to her, but nobody was paying her any attention. They all looked like they were in a deep conversation with God. Some were sitting in their seats, while others were sitting around the front with their eyes closed. Some people were standing with their hands raised, while others covered their faces and wept. She looked to see what the pastor was doing and found him kneeling at the front crying out to God. Anna was overwhelmed by a desire to go to the altar and pray. She snuck a glance over at Alex and the peace she saw on him as he lifted his hands and worshiped made the tears that she was fighting so hard begin to fall. Quietly she slipped past him and, as if being led, slowly made her way to the front. Once there, she knelt down and before she could even try to think of any words to say she started to weep.

She was overwhelmed with such a loving peace that she could hardly believe it. How could a God so big step off His throne for her? She was nobody. She had never done anything remarkable. Nonetheless, she felt as though she was being completely embraced by His love. She was too afraid to pray out loud, so she spoke in her head and hoped that He heard her.

"God, I don't know how to pray anymore. I know I used to when I was little, but that was before…Well, before my childhood got ripped away. I know I act like it never happened and that it doesn't bother me, but it's because I have to. I had to be strong just to survive the pain of everything that I've been through. I don't know how not to be strong. I have this wall around my heart that I pretend will protect me from being hurt. I don't know how to really let anyone fully past my defenses. But Jesus, I really want to. I want to be able to give my heart to You fully and have complete trust that You will never hurt me. Please, God, break down my walls."

She must have sat there crying and praying for hours. Or at least that's how it felt when she was finally finished and looked around. She thought for sure that she would be the only one still there but was surprised and happy to see people still praying all around the altar. She looked to her right and was filled with love all over again when she saw that Alex had come up and prayed with her. She could see that he had been crying and wasn't ashamed by it. She fell completely in love with him right then and there. Maybe God had already started breaking down her walls, because before she prayed, she only thought she might love him but was too afraid to fully surrender to it. But after she prayed, when she looked at him, she was overwhelmed with loving him, with wanting to be with him, to stay with him.

"I love you," she said before she thought about it.

He looked almost as shocked as she felt. He loved her already, but every time they had talked about it, she would always say that she wasn't ready for a deep relationship like that. Just yesterday she was saying that she cared for him but had been through too much in her life to be able to commit to something as deep as love. He was a little saddened by the thought that she didn't love him like he did her but was willing to keep trying because he loved her so much. He looked deep into her eyes for a long moment, tears filling his once again. He pulled her in his arms and hugged her with every fiber of his being. "I love you, too. So, so much."

156

Chapter 24

"I'm glad I came with you tonight," Anna said on their way home.

He took his eyes off the road for a quick moment to smile at her. "Me too."

She sat quietly for another minute while working up the nerve to say what was on her mind. "I didn't know it would feel like that."

"What did it feel like to you?" he asked, wanting to hear her view on how it felt to be touched by the Holy Spirit.

"I don't know… freeing? Like I was being held… surrounded… cherished, I think, is the best word I can find for it. Like no matter what my past was, I was completely and fully accepted. Loved." She turned in her seat to face him. "Does that make sense?"

He chuckled softly. "Absolutely. I feel that same way every time I pray." He gave her a quick glance. "And the best thing is that you don't have to wait until Sunday to feel that."

"What do you mean?"

"God is with us all the time. He doesn't just wait at church for us to talk to Him. He is wherever we are. He lives inside of us. Even before we come to Him for the first time, He is there; just waiting for us to acknowledge Him."

She thought on that for a moment. "At every time in our lives?"

"Yes," he answered as he pulled up in front of her house.

She didn't get out. Instead, she stared at her house in silence.

"Are you ok?"

She must have been deep in thought, because when he placed his hand on her shoulder she about jumped out of her seat.

"What? Um, yes. I just-- I was just thinking about something."

"What about?"

She turned back to him and the love that she saw in his eyes told her that she could talk to him about anything, but she still had to ask. "Can I talk to you about something?"

"Yes," he said after only a moment's pause.

She saw the flicker of fear in his face but pushed on. "So, you said that God is always there and always has been, right?"

"Yeah."

"What about when bad things happen? Horrible, unspeakable things. Is He there then?"

He took a slow breath in, praying that he would say the right words. "Always."

"Then why does He let bad things happen?"

"Well," he said another quick mental prayer, "God is not a dictator. He is a loving and faithful God. He wants people to follow Him because they love Him, not because they have to."

"Ok, but wouldn't it be easier for people to trust Him if He protected them from crappy stuff?"

"I don't think so. I think that if nothing hard ever came our way, we probably wouldn't talk to God as much. I hate to say it, but a lot of people only talk to Him when they need something. Jesus loves us so much that He wants to talk to us all the time, not just when things are hard. If we are in commune with Him during the good times, when the hard times hit, it's a little easier, emotionally and mentally. You know what I mean?"

"I guess. But that doesn't make it any easier to forget the bad, though."

"No, it doesn't make it easier to forget, but it makes it easier to get through. Knowing that we have a Father who loves us enough to die for us, and who wants to be with us no matter the things we do. Or have done *to* us." He didn't know why he felt led to say that last part; he just knew that he had to.

Anna was stunned. She sat there staring as hot tears started falling down her face. "Why did you say it like that?" she whispered.

He lowered his voice to match hers. "I don't know. I felt like that's what God wanted me to say." He could see that she was fighting an internal battle, so he reached out and took her hand. "You know that I love you, right?"

"Yes."

"There is nothing that would ever change that. Nothing."

"I think I want to tell you something."

"You can tell me anything."

She took a deep breath and told him about her past. All the abuse that she had to face, her dad's death, and her sister's part in it. By the time she was done, she was crying in earnest.

He pulled her close and rested his chin on her head. He didn't say anything for a few minutes, just held her as she cried. Through his own tears he said, "I am so, so sorry that happened to you. I wish I could take a magic wand and undo it all so that you would never have to have gone through that."

She sniffled into his chest. "I was so angry. Angry at the men, angry at my sister, angry at my mom. I think I was even angry at God. I couldn't understand why He had let all that stuff happen. That's why I was so hesitant to go to church with you. When we first started dating, I knew that you went to church, and I was dreading the day when you would ask me to go with you. I was actually surprised you waited so long." She pulled back to look in his eyes. "Why *did* you wait so long?"

"I don't know. The timing just never felt right."

She thought on that before responding, "Do you think that was God's doing?"

"Probably. He usually knows what He's doing." He winked at her and gave a small smile.

She smiled back. "He must, because I think if you would have asked me before, I probably would have said no."

"Well, I, for one, am glad you said yes."

"Me too."

A Secret Well Kept

Chapter 25

"Merry Christmas, Alex! Come in," Melissa said opening the door and wrapping Alex in a hug. "How is work going?"

"It's good." He gave her a kiss on the cheek. Smiling, he winked and said, "Busy, as I'm sure Anna has probably complained to you about."

Anna walked in just in time to hear him say that. She playfully punched him on the shoulder. "You know I don't complain about that."

He grabbed her by the waist and pulled her against him for a quick kiss. "I know, I'm just teasing. I'm the one who's always complaining. I don't get to see you nearly as much as I want to. Today is the first day in two weeks that I got to put my arms around you." He nuzzled his face into her neck.

She laughed as she pulled away and tugged him into the living room. "Yeah, I do miss that, but we talk every day."

He pulled her in for another hug. "Not the same as getting to see your beautiful face."

They stood there in each other's embrace just basking in the love they had for each other.

"I do have some good news."

Sitting down on the couch she asked, "What?"

"I talked to my sergeant yesterday and asked him if I could start getting off every Sunday for church and he agreed."

"That is so awesome! I hated that you have only been able to come every other week. It helps that my mom started going with me, but it's not the same without you."

"Gee, thanks," Melissa teased, coming into the room with a glass of eggnog for Alex.

"You know what I mean, mom." Anna smiled at her mom. She truly was happy that her mom had come to know the same Love that she had.

"I know." She winked at her daughter. "Ok, so now that Alex is here, I say we open presents *before* we eat."

"What? That's a change. Usually, you make us wait until after dessert."

She looked conspiratorially at Alex. "Yeah, well I'm changing things up this year. I'm the mom, so I'm allowed."

"Ok." She looked over at Alex who was busy pulling gifts from his bag. "I'll go first." She jumped up and knelt in front of the tree. She pulled out a small rectangular gift with a big purple ribbon on it. "Mom."

Melissa took the gift and began unwrapping. "Oh!" She exclaimed when she opened it to find a sparkling silver chain with a beautiful emerald hanging on it.

"It's a mother's necklace."

Melissa's smile fell for the briefest of moments. She wanted to ask about Liza's birthstone, but she knew Anna didn't like to talk about her. The last time they did, Anna had said that she forgave Liza because she had to, but she would never claim her as a sister. "Thank you, baby. I love it."

"Your turn," she said as she tossed a box the size of a book to Alex, who had moved to sit on the couch.

He peeled off the blue bow and placed it on his head before tearing the wrapping paper. He opened the box to reveal a picture frame with a poem written over-top of a picture of the two of them. He started to read it silently when Melissa told him she wanted to hear it, since her daughter refused to tell her what she had gotten him.

He looked at the two of them and smiled. "Ok."

"How do you define love?
How do you give it an explanation?
Do you use big words that have deep meaning?
Do you use small words full of emotion?

Love is the moon that smiles down
when everything else is dark.
The stars that light up the night sky.

Love is the brilliant colors of a single rainbow
after a raging storm.
The rays of sunshine that escape from behind the
dark clouds.

Love is the river that carries hope
to the desert lands.
The lake that cools down a hot summer's day.

Love is the tree that provides shelter
from the heat of the sun.
The flower that gives beauty to everything around
it.

Love is lying down in your bed at the end of a long,
hard day.
The faith that you cling to when everything is
going bad.

How do I define love?
It's the beat that my heart skips
when I open my phone and see a text from you.

It's the smile on my lips when I'm thinking about
you.

It's the twinkle in my eyes when I am looking into
yours.

Love is us, me and you,
now and forever
and always."

He set the picture gently in his lap and stared at it for a second longer. When he finally looked up there were tears in his eyes. "That was absolutely beautiful." He walked over to the tree, knelt next to Anna and gave her a gentle kiss. "I love you."

"I love you too." She waited a beat before she jumped up and said, "Since you are already down there, you can go next." She joined her mom on the couch.

"Ok." He pulled out a package and handed it to Melissa. "You first."

She accepted the red wrapped box. She took her time opening it. She pulled out a leather-bound study bible with her name engraved on it. "Alex, thank you. I love it. I was just telling Anna a while ago that I needed to get myself a bible."

He winked at her. "I know, she told me." Everyone laughed.

"Well, I'm glad to see she remembered."

He turned to look under the tree for Anna's gift. He stayed down for a moment longer, searching. "Hmm." He turned to her with concern on his face. "I thought I put your gift down here but I can't find it. Will you help me look?"

She rolled her eyes playfully. "Men," she said to her mom as she passed. She knelt down and started looking. When she didn't see it, she stood up and said as much.

He turned to face her. "I thought for sure I brought it. I'm sorry, I will have to get it when we leave."

She just laughed and played with the bow that was still on his head. "That's fine, hon'. You'll just have to be my gift." Smiling, she turned to sit back down.

"If you'll have me, I will be," he said, reaching out and grabbing her hand.

"Wha--" She couldn't finish her question because the moment she turned back around her eyes were instantly focused on the small, black velvet box sitting open in his hand, a twinkling diamond ring nestled perfectly inside.

"I would love to be your gift every day for the rest of our lives, if you would do me the greatest honor in the world and be my wife."

She raised her hand to her mouth and bit down on her knuckles to keep herself from crying, or rather from bawling like a baby. The tears were already falling down her cheeks. She couldn't get her voice to work so she nodded.

He stood up and took her left hand. "Yes?"

Still nodding, she was finally able to make herself speak. "Yes. Yes!" She threw her arms around his neck and held on tight. "Yes!"

"Good, 'cause I don't know if the store has a return policy," he said, laughing as he pulled away enough to slip the ring onto her finger.

She took a moment to look at it again and then turned to show her mom. "Look at--" She stopped talking when she noticed her mom holding her cell phone, recording everything. "Wait." She looked back and forth between the two of them. "Mom, did you know about this already?"

"Of course I did."

"I asked her permission before I bought the ring," Alex filled in.

Tearing up again she laughed and hugged first Alex then her mom. "I love you."

"I love you, too." she said, wiping away tears of her own. She was so happy that Anna had such a wonderful man who respected her and her dreams. Someone who would support her more than just financially. Pulling back, she said, "Ok, I'll pass out my gifts then we can eat."

Chapter 26

"You look stunning, baby," Anna's Uncle Frank said when he met her at the back of the sanctuary. Since her dad couldn't be there, her uncle said that he would be honored to walk her down the aisle.

"Thank you." She couldn't believe how fast time was going by. It seemed like just yesterday she was walking across campus and tripping over her future husband's legs. Then she blinked and they were engaged. She blinked again and here she was, about to give her life to the best man she had ever met.

She wished her dad could be there to see the woman she became. She hoped that he would be proud of her. Of everything she had overcome. Of finishing three years of college so far. Of marrying a great guy. With that thought of Alex, she stopped thinking about anything else. As she started down the aisle, she had eyes and thoughts only for him.

Alex stood at the front of the church, surrounded by their family and friends, and had to hold back the tears when he saw Anna. She was an angel in white walking towards him. It felt like everyone else disappeared and there was only her. He hoped that when the time came, he could remember the vows he wrote for her.

"Alex, would you like to read your vows first?" Pastor Brent asked.

He glanced towards him quickly and said yes before returning his gaze to his beautiful bride. "Anna, words cannot express how very happy I am at this moment, which is why I had such a hard time writing these vows." He smiled and winked at her while everyone in the room laughed. She smiled back as he continued. "I know it's not usual for a man to admit to dreaming about his wedding and future wife all his life, but that was me. I have dreamt of finding the perfect bride my entire life. I just knew that God was going to give me this amazing woman who would be my helpmate, my confidant, my best friend; one that would always be there to lift me up when my faith is waning. A person that would love me when I am being my awesome charming self, and even more when I am a grouchy bear of a man. When we first met, I can't say that I knew right then and there that you would one day be my wife. Heck, if I'm honest I didn't even think you would be my girlfriend. I remember feeling awestruck at how beautiful you looked that day you tripped over me. I never thought there would be a chance for someone so lovely as you and the slob I'm sure you thought I was. I didn't know our future, but I did know that I wanted there to be one. That day was the best day of my life up until then. Each day after with you has only gotten better. I can't wait to spend the rest of my life with you, showing you every day how very blessed I am to be your husband. I vow to carry you to our room when you fall asleep on the couch. I vow to do my share of the housework, without too much grumbling. I vow to be the kind of man that you deserve. The kind of man who is willing to put you first. Today, before our family and friends, I declare that I will strive to always be the God-fearing man that loves his wife more than his own life. Forever and always, and maybe a little longer." He winked at her again.

She took a deep breath in, trying to control the tears that welled up in her eyes at his words. She chuckled a little when she lifted her hand up to catch one that escaped. Exhaling, she started, "Alex, I wish I could say that I *was* that little girl who always dreamed about their wedding day, but I would be lying. I never dreamt of my wedding day because I never thought I would get married. I never believed that there was a man out there that would love me the way I needed to be loved. And then I tripped over you. Or rather, fell for you. You were smart and cute, and you had a way of making me laugh at the littlest thing. You weren't afraid to be yourself and showed me that it was ok for me to do the same. You have helped me overcome some of the fears that once kept me from believing in love. I thank God that He has given me such a wonderful man. This day I vow to be everything that you need me to be. I vow to never hide. I vow to pray for you every day. I vow to rub your shoulders when the load is too heavy. I vow to never give up."

Alex wiped the tears that fell down his cheeks. "I love you," he mouthed.

"I love you," she whispered back.

"You may kiss your bride."

Alex did not hesitate to pull Anna in and kiss her with all the love that was overflowing in his heart. The crowd erupted in claps and shouts, but they didn't hear it over their love for each other.

Chapter 27

"Ok, that's the last of this load," Alex said as he set down the last box. "Me and Mick are going to go load the rest of it."

"Ok." She stopped unpacking the pots and pans to give him a kiss. "I love you."

He smiled. "I love you, too." He kissed her before turning back to the living room. "Hey, Frank, thanks again for helping out. Do you wanna drive with me and Mick to load up the last bunch?"

Frank looked around at all the boxes that were scattered around. "No, I think I'll stay here. Maybe me and Anna can have a lot of this put where it belongs before you get back."

"Ok, we'll be back then." He waved and walked out the door.

"Thank you for helping Uncle Frank. You really didn't need to, but we do appreciate it," Anna said carrying a cup of water in for him.

"I'm glad to help my favorite niece."

"I'm your only niece." She looked around the room, trying not to get overwhelmed at how much there was to do. "So, where do we start? I was working so long in the kitchen that I didn't realize all this was still out here."

"Let's start opening boxes to find out which room they belong in. Then we can take and line them up along the walls."

"Sounds like a plan."

They started opening boxes and carrying them to where they needed to be. She directed him as they worked together until all the boxes were in the appropriate rooms.

"Wow!" She said after looking at the time. "That only took us about thirty minutes." She shot a quick text to Alex. When he replied she continued, "Alex said they won't be back for at least another hour. Do you want to take a break while I start unpacking my bedroom?"

"Sure." He followed her into her room and plopped down on the bed. Putting his hands behind his head, he laid back and said, "Comfy bed."

She looked over from the closet. "Is it? Alex told me how much he liked it, but I haven't tried it out yet."

"No time like the present," he said patting the space next to him.

She hesitated, her mind instantly going back to the men in her past that hurt her. She tried her hardest to never think about it, but once in a while something would happen, or someone would say something that would hit her so forcefully that the mental shield she had placed around her past would fall, and she would revert back to that little girl who was afraid that every man wanted to hurt her. She and Alex had many conversations about it before the wedding. She wanted to tell him everything that she still struggled with on a daily basis, even if nobody could see it. She told him how sometimes when a man simply smiles at her she has a battle in her mind. A part of her brain is always saying that he was only being nice to her because he was trying to get something from her. The logical part told her he wasn't, that he was just being a nice man and had no hidden agenda. She told him how some of the littlest phrases, comments or actions would send her reeling back mentally and the battle would begin again. She told him how she had to erect her mental forcefield every single morning just to make it through the day. She smiled when she remembered what he had replied. He had said that he would do anything and everything he could to never give her cause to doubt that he didn't want anything from her but her love.

She shook her head mentally and came back to the present. "I think I'm going to finish these boxes up first."

"Ok, your loss. This bed is great."

She turned back to the boxes and unpacked four big boxes before she had to stop and stretch her back.

"Bet you'd like that break now," Frank said chuckling.

She looked at him dubiously. She battled for a half a second, but finally made up in her mind to believe that this was her Uncle Frank, he was not those other men. She couldn't put their crimes on him. That was what she had to tell herself with other men in the past when the thoughts came into her head. Not everyone was like those men from her childhood, and she wasn't a child anymore.

Putting her fears behind her she said, "I think I will." She practically fell onto the bed. After a minute of lying there with her eyes closed, she said, "Wow, this is a crazy comfortable bed. Alex has good taste." She looked over at her uncle only to find him lying on his side looking at her. *Was he a little closer than he was before?* A niggling of panic started to make its way up her stomach, but she swallowed it back down thinking, *No. He's my uncle. He isn't going to do anything; I'm just being paranoid like, always.* She turned her head back away and closed her eyes, fighting to keep the unwanted thoughts from infiltrating her mind. Just as she was getting some control over them, she stopped breathing when she felt his hand reach over and touch her hair.

Her body was completely paralyzed with fear, but her brain was screaming. *Why is he touching my hair? That's just a weird thing for an uncle to do. What should I do? Pretend to be asleep and hope he stops? Tell him to stop? No. No, it's ok. I'm being paranoid. He's just smoothing the hair off my face, nothing like before. It's ok.*

She almost started to believe it was when she felt his hand brush the side of her face. She squeezed her eyes closed a little harder. *No, no, no.* She wanted to tell him to stop but couldn't. She was no longer in control of herself, instead, her six-year-old self had taken over. She wanted to scream for him to stop when she felt his hand glide down her neck to the upper part of her chest and with each circling caress, move his hand lower until he was touching the upper part of her breasts just above her tank top. She tried to scream, but the only thing she heard was the voice in her head saying, *"Don't say anything. You can't. What if they get mad?"* The scared little girl in her head kept repeating it over and over again.

He leaned closer and started kissing on her shoulder. After what felt like an eternity, she heard him whisper, "Is this ok?"

Those words were enough for her adult self to take back some control, not much, but enough to mumble, "I would really prefer you not."

She almost wept with relief when his hand stopped moving, then he removed it altogether. She still dared not to open her eyes but was overjoyed when he started to get up.

"I have to go pick up some stuff from the store before it gets too late. Do you need anything?" he asked from the door.

"No." She was barely able to talk above a whisper.

"Ok, I'll see you later."

She lay there without breathing until she heard the front door shut. Then she started crying and didn't stop until sleep overtook her.

"Anna. Hey, sweetheart, wake up." Alex said. He sat on the side of the bed and was rubbing her shoulder.

She opened her eyes and was so relieved to see him that she threw herself into his arms and tried not to break down.

He held her silently until she pulled away to lay back down. "We got the rest of the stuff in, and Mick is taking the truck back to mom's. You slept through it all. Is everything ok?"

She looked around the room before she answered. "Yeah, it's just-- I think I did too much today. Would it be horribly bad if we just leave the stuff for tomorrow and go to bed early tonight?"

"Of course not, sweetie. I'll go lock up and be right back."

She wanted to tell him what had happened, but how could she? She felt so ashamed. She was not a little child who couldn't defend herself, she was an adult. Why didn't she stand up for herself? Why did it take so long for her to finally ask him to stop? Thoughts like these bombarded her brain until she fell asleep again.

A Secret Well Kept

Chapter 28

Two days later they had just finished dinner and were about to watch a movie when Anna said, "Alex, can I talk to you about something?"

"Sure, what's up?" He placed the popcorn on the table and settled back on the couch next to her.

She didn't know where to begin. She wanted to tell him what had happened, had to tell him. Yet she wasn't sure that she should. What if he got upset with her? What if he told her it was all her fault? She clamped down on her fears for the thousandth time. He loved her. She was being ridiculous.

"I need to tell you something, but I need your word that you won't get upset."

He looked at her intently. "Should I be scared?"

"No." She took his hand. "But what I have to tell you is hard for me to say. Also, I want your word that you will keep it between the two of us. Ok?"

"Ok," he said skeptically.

Haltingly she told him about what had happened when they were moving in.

"What?! Why didn't you tell me right away? I would have arrested him for assault right then." Alex got up and started pacing the floor after she finished her story. He was furious.

"I-- I just-- I don't know. I was afraid." She didn't face him. She had told him everything while staring at her hands, and she still couldn't look at him.

He stopped pacing, sat down next to her and took her hands. "Afraid of what? Me?" he asked.

She looked up into his eyes then, shocked. "What? No. Never. Why would you think that?"

"I don't know who else you would be afraid of."

"It's not that I was afraid of you, more like I was afraid of your reaction." She continued before he could ask another question, "I think I was afraid that maybe you would blame me for what happened."

"*You?* How could that possibly be your fault?"

"I don't know. I know it's not rational, that's why I'm telling you now. I've been going back and forth on saying anything, but today I decided that you needed to know; that I didn't want there to be any secrets between us."

He leaned over to pick up his cell phone. "Ok, well, now that I do know, I can have him arrest for assault."

"Wait, no. You can't!" She snatched the phone from his hand and stood up.

He stood up with her. "What do you mean I can't? He assaulted you, my *wife*. I'm a cop and you think I'm not going to arrest him? He'd better be glad that's *all* I'm going to do to him."

She touched his arm. "Please. You can't arrest him. You said we would keep this just between us. You gave your word." She knew she was hitting below the belt with that, but she needed him to not say anything. She needed to know that he was, indeed, going to keep this quiet.

"That's not fair."

"I know, and I'm sorry."

"Why? Why wouldn't you want him arrested?"

"Because. He didn't do anything that *really* hurt me. And more than that, my mom has been through enough in the past fifteen years, I don't want to add to it."

He looked at her incredulously. "How would him getting arrested hurt her?"

"She just reconnected with her family after my dad died. She loves her brother. I can't take him away from her after everything she's already lost."

He stared at her for a long moment before saying, "Fine. Even though this goes against everything I know should happen, I won't say anything." She visibly relaxed. "Under two conditions."

She tried to guess what his conditions would be.

"One, I never want to see him again. He is never to step foot in our house, ever."

"Ok, I agree with that. Never would be too soon."

"And two, I want you to confront him on what he did."

"What?! No! I can't do that. You know I can't."

"That's my condition."

She knew he wasn't doing it to be mean, but that didn't make it any easier. "Why? Why do I have to confront him?"

"Because, when you were a child and those things happened, you never got to tell them how it made you feel. You were too young and afraid. This time, you're not."

"But I am. I am afraid. I don't know if I can."

"You can." He walked up and took her by the shoulders. Looking deep in her eyes he said, "You are one of the bravest people I know. The stuff you've been through would have destroyed most people. Instead, here you are. Married, happy, I hope, and one year away from graduating college. You are a lot stronger than you give yourself credit for. If you want, I will be with you when you do."

"Can I do it over the phone?" she asked in a resigned whisper.

"Yes. Do you want me to stay with you?"

She thought about it for a minute but decided that he was right. She did need to confront him, even if over the phone, and that she needed to do it alone. "No, that's ok. I think I can do it myself."

He leaned in and kissed her on the forehead. "I know you can. I'll be in the other room. If you need me, just holler."

She nodded and he walked away. She sat down on the couch and stared at the phone for a full minute before finally making the call.

"Hello," her uncle answered.

"Uncle Frank?"

"Yeah. Is that you Anna?"

"Yes."

"Hey, honey. How are you liking your new place?"

She could hear the smile in his voice, and it made her grind her teeth. How dare he be happy after what he did. Did he think that she had forgotten already? "I need to talk to you."

"Ok, what's up?" He still sounded like he didn't have a care in the world.

"You hurt me. I was supposed to be able to trust you and you hurt me instead. You should never have touched me like you did. It wasn't right."

He was silent for a moment before replying, "You're an adult."

She was perplexed by his statement. "What does that have to do with anything?"

"Just as I said, I'm not a child molester like your father's brother? At least I waited until you were an adult to try something."

She let out a quick exhale. Was he serious? Did he really think that made what he did ok?

"It was still wrong. I no longer trust you and I no longer want you around us. I will forgive you for what you did, but as of right now, I never want to see you again."

She hung up before she started crying. Alex heard and rushed in the room. Taking her in his arms he rocked her and asked if she was ok.

"I am. That was hard, but I'm glad you made me do it." She told him about the conversation.

"Are you serious? That was really his response?"

"Yeah. Pretty messed up, right?"

"All I'm saying is that he is lucky I made a promise to a beautiful lady whom I love. Otherwise… I'm not even going to start on what all I would do." He looked down at the table and the popcorn sitting on it. "Do you still want to watch a movie?"

She plopped down on the couch and pulled him down next to her. "Absolutely. No more worrying about stupid people for the day."

"Agreed." He kissed her, grabbed the remote, and started the movie.

A Secret Well Kept

Chapter 29

"I can't believe I finally made it!" Anna exclaimed when she finally made her way through the crowd to her mom and Alex. She hugged them both before saying, "Now all I want to do is get out of here. Who's hungry?"

She led the way to the car. "I'm craving some serious Chinese. Golden Dragon sound good to you guys?"

"Today is your day, sweetheart, so whatever you want is what I want," Melissa said giving her another hug.

"And I will eat anything," Alex said as he opened the door for them.

"So, do you have any plans for working?" Melissa asked before taking a bite of sushi.

"Not yet. I think I might stay home for a while, take some time off."

Alex reached over and took her hand. "And I, for one, can't wait. I am going to love not sharing you for a while."

Anna smiled at him when she noticed Melissa set down her piece of sushi. "Mom, are you ok? You always eat a lot of sushi, but you barely ate one."

"I'm fine. My stomach has just been a little upset the past couple days. It's ok. Let's just enjoy this moment. The day my baby became a doctor."

"I'm not a doctor, mom." She loved that her mom believed in her so much. "It's a bachelor's in psychology. I'm thinking about working in social services or something."

"Whatever. Same thing to me. I'm still the proudest mama on the planet. I--" she was cut off by a coughing fit. Regaining her breath, she took a sip of water. "Sorry, must have gone down the wrong pipe."

Anna looked at Alex then back to her mom. "Mom, are you sure you're alright? I've noticed that in the past few days you've been a lot quieter than usual."

Melissa looked them both in the eyes and determined that she would not be able to talk her way out of this conversation. "Can we go and talk about this at home?"

They nodded in unison and left the restaurant.

"Ok. What's going on?" Anna asked the moment they walked in the door.

"Alex, would you like something to drink?"

"No, tha--"

"Don't change the subject. I know something's wrong, just tell me."

"Ok, you're right. Something is wrong, but I didn't want to tell you today. I wanted this day to be all about you. What I have to say can keep."

"No, it can't. You know that I will just start thinking about every possible thing that could be wrong, so you might as well tell me and save me from the mental anguish."

Melissa took a deep, fortifying breath before starting her story. "A few weeks ago, I was at my annual doctor's appointment when she found something."

"What?" Anna asked when her mom didn't continue.

"She found a lump." She paused again. "She sent me to have a biopsy done and the results came back positive."

"Ok. Ok. So, what do we do next? How are we going to fight this? Have you been to get a second opinion anywhere?" The protective, take control side of Anna rushed out in a wave.

Melissa lifted her hands to stop her. "Wait, there's more. But to answer your questions, yes, I have gotten a second opinion and the next step is to discuss exactly what treatment plan I will be doing. But you need to know something. It's pretty bad."

They stared at each other for a long moment.

"How bad?" Anna whispered.

"Stage four. I'm waiting for the tests to come back to see how far the cancer has spread, but things aren't looking too good right now."

"When did you have the other tests done?"

She looked away. "Yesterday."

"Mom! Why didn't you tell me? I would have gone with you. For that matter, why didn't you tell me when you first found out?"

She raised her head and looked straight into Anna's eyes. "Because I didn't want to put this burden on you. You had finals and then you had to prepare for graduation. I didn't want my problems interfering."

"This is not a 'burden that would be placed on me.' You are my mom, and I would do anything for you."

"I know that, which is exactly why I didn't tell you. I knew that you would have skipped classes and tests just to go with me to the doctor's appointments. Then you would have not been able to graduate on time, and I couldn't have that on my conscience. Please, don't be upset. I just wanted your graduation to be perfect. I'm sorry I had to ruin it with bad news. I was trying my hardest not to let anything show."

Anna walked over and wrapped her arms protectively around her. "You are a wonderful mom. I could never be upset with you, especially when you were just trying to protect me. But from here on out, don't. You will have enough to deal with in kicking this cancer's butt. It's my turn to protect you, mom. I love you so much." She straightened her shoulders and pulled Melissa back far enough to look in her eyes. Determinedly she said, "We'll get through this. You're going to be ok. Everything is going to be just fine."

Epilogue

"Hey, Mom," Anna said, walking over to give her mom a kiss on the cheek. "How are you feeling today?"

"Tired," Melissa replied.

The surgery to remove the cancer went more smoothly than any of them had hoped, even the doctor was surprised. No sooner than she felt like she was feeling better from the surgery, she had started radiation. Anna came every day to take her. She had wanted to move in, but Melissa refused. She argued that Anna and Alex needed to have their own space, that she would be fine. After hours of arguing, Anna conceded under the stipulation that she be there to take her to every doctor's appointment.

"Well, why don't you go nap and I'll start cleaning? I think I'll finally work on cleaning out my old room."

"You know you don't have to clean every day, right?"

"I know." She bent over, gave her mom another kiss and turned to walk away before her mom could argue more.

An hour and a half later, Anna was finishing the closet when something hidden behind a pile of clothes on the top shelf caught her eye. Pushing the clothes out of the way she froze; she recognized that rainbow swirl design. It was Liza's journal. She could remember asking Liza why she was always writing in it. Her reply was always the same, "So when I'm older I can remember all the details." Anna didn't need a journal for that. She remembered very clearly the most important detail about Liza, that she killed her dad. She wanted to take it to the backyard and burn it. She grabbed it and slammed it to the ground, all her feelings of anger and hatred taking control. Jumping down off the chair that she was using, she stalked over and had every intention of burning it, but as she was reaching her hand down, her eyes caught upon her name. She stood up and pulled her hand away like she had been burned.

After a few calming breaths, she decided that she had to read it. She had to, in order to have a sense of closure. She hesitantly picked it up, still staring at it like it was a coiled snake about to bite, and bite it did.

Anna first checked on her mom, who was still sleeping in her bed, then sat down on the couch to read. She flipped through the pages, thinking she would just glimpse through it, when a folded piece of paper fell out. Her heart stammered a little when she opened it to find a letter addressed to her.

Dear Anna,

> *I know you will never forgive me for what I plan to do this weekend, but it's something I have to do. I want you to know that I love you more than life itself and would do anything within my power to protect you. I know you probably hate me, but if you read my journal, I hope that you will understand. I know I've always told you that you were not allowed to read it, but I will make an exception this time. I want you to know that you have been the best little sister I could have ever asked for. I really wish there was another way to protect you, but I can't think of one.*

Anna almost flung the letter away with that. Really? Protect her? Is that what Liza calls murder?

> *There are so many things that happened that made me come to my*

decision. I never wanted to tell you any of what you are about to read, but I also never want you to hate me. I want you to be mad about the choice I had to make, but not at me. And that will never happen unless you read my story. So please, Anna, read it. And know that everything I ever did was for you.

I love you to the moon and back, my little French fry.

Love Always,
Liza

Anna rolled her eyes and tossed the letter to the side. She picked up the journal and decided to just read it from beginning to end. She took a break after reading about how Liza helped decorate for her sixth birthday. She went in to find her mom awake and sitting up in her bed.

"Hey, you're up."

"Yeah," Melissa said. "I thought about getting some lunch, but I'm not really hungry."

"You sure? I could go make you a sandwich or something."

"I'm sure, honey. I think I'll just sit here and watch some *Wheel of Fortune* or something."

"Ok, well, I'll be in the living room. If you need me, just holler." She closed the door softly and walked back to the couch.

She picked up the journal and started where she left off. She had just read about Liza teaching her to skate right before she turned seven when she sucked in her breath. No. She reread the entry three more times, refusing to believe what was written.

I didn't write this the other day because I just couldn't believe that it really happened. Why would dad ever do something like that? I thought for sure that Anna knew that something had happened when she came outside and found me hiding. I'm glad she didn't ask many questions about it. I hoped it wouldn't happen again, but I hoped wrong. I don't know. I think maybe I thought the other day was a onetime thing, like a mistake. But then dad came in to get me at bedtime. Anna wanted to come too, but that was because she didn't know what was going to happen. Dad took me into his office and closed the door. I wanted to scream when he came closer and made me take my shirt off. I tried to tell him no, but he grabbed my arm and told me to shut up and do what I was told. Then he started rubbing on me. I wanted to vomit. I still do. I think I must have mumbled that a dad should not be doing something like that because he pinched me and said that a daughter was supposed to do what the parents say, not question them.

Anna wanted to vomit. There was no way this was true. Her dad would never have done anything like what Liza was saying. She didn't want to continue reading, but at the same time, she knew she had to. There was something pushing her to keep going, to find out what else Liza was going to say. She read passage after passage. Read how Liza said her dad threatened that if Liza ever said anything, nobody would believe her. That since he was a lawyer, he knew how to make things go his way. He said that he would be able to prove that Liza was an unstable girl who loved to make up stories. That he was a well-known and respected adult and that she was just a child, nobody would listen to her. She read that he had started hurting her in more ways than just rape. That sometimes he would point his gun at her and threaten to shoot her if she didn't do everything he told her to; and what he made her do made Anna almost vomit. She didn't realize she'd been crying until she got to the last passage and couldn't catch her breath. She sat the journal down for a moment to wipe her face. She was determined to finish what she had started.

> *I made a decision. Anna won't be at George's this weekend, and neither will his girlfriend. He says he has big plans, but I know what kind of plans he has. And I am done with them. I'm going to end this once and for all. I will NOT give him the chance to hurt Anna the way he has me. He says that she is growing up, but I know what that means for him. He thinks that he will be able to start hurting her. I won't allow that. My life is ruined, but I will not let him ruin hers. I missed my period this month. I know what that means. He put his monster in me. I also know that I can't let him hurt Anna. Her life is not going to be like mine was, if I can help it. I will never be able to see my little sister grow up, but at least I can make sure she does without this kind of pain. This will be my final entry, because tomorrow, after I shoot him, I am going to shoot myself. I won't be able to live after I*

kill him. Anna and mom would hate me, and they wouldn't understand that I did it for them. I know George is a liar, but I believe him when he tells me that if I ever told anyone they wouldn't believe me. I hope that one day Anna and mom will forgive me, but either way, I will do what I have to do to protect my family.

"Sweetheart, what's wrong?" Melissa asked folding her arms around Anna.

She must have zoned off crying and staring blankly at the journal. She hadn't even heard her mom walk in the room. Too many thoughts were going through her head for her to focus on any one. When she felt her mom's arms wrap around her, the dam broke and the tears that were falling slowly down her face started raining down in earnest.

"Oh, mom!" she sobbed. "It's horrible!" After a full five minutes of crying, Anna calmed down enough to say, "I found Liza's journal."

Melissa sucked in her breath. Anna had not said her sister's name in so many years. "Yeah?"

"Mom," she turned to look into Melissa eyes. "What she says in here, it can't be true. It just can't."

She looked down at the journal then back up. "What does it say?"

Anna just shook her head. "I can't. I can't say what's in here." She handed it to her. "You read it. I'm going to go sit out on the back porch."

An hour and a half later Melissa joined her outside. When Anna looked over, she knew that she had been crying, too. Her face was streaked and blotchy. She didn't say anything, instead she took her mom in her arms and they sat there quietly crying together.

Finally, Anna pulled back and asked the question that had been niggling at her. "Mom, do you think all that was true? Do you think dad really did what Liza said he did?"

"I want to say no, because that would mean that I let him hurt one of my babies. But..."

"But what?"

"Anna, honey, your dad was not a nice man."

She took a step back. "What do you mean? He was always nice from what I can remember."

"He was pretty nice to you girls, and now I find out just *how* nice." She paused to calm herself back down. She was so angry about what she'd read. It was all she could do not to hate herself for what happened but knew that would do no good for either of them. "He--he wasn't so nice to me."

"What? Why didn't you ever say anything?"

"Because, before you were too little, and then he was gone so I didn't see the point."

Anna stared at her mom for a long moment before asking, "What did he do?"

Melissa sighed. "He used to hurt me, physically and emotionally. If I contradicted him in any way, he would wait until you girls were in bed and then he would hurt me. Sometimes it was pinching, hitting... choking. And the things he would say to me. I can't even bare to repeat them."

"Why did you stay with him then?" she whispered.

She took Anna by the hand and led her to the porch swing. "Let's sit down and I will tell you, everything."

"When I was fifteen my parents got divorced. My dad left and never called or saw us again. My mom was distraught. She pretty much stopped caring what your aunt, uncle and I did. My dad was always so strict and controlling that we were never allowed to do anything. After he left, well, Aunt Meg kind of went wild. She took full advantage of my mom's complacency. I never really wanted to go out like she did, but one day she talked me into it. It was a night I would never forget. She wanted me to go to a party with her, but I refused. After hours of her begging, I finally agreed. I didn't like it there. Everyone was drinking and doing all kinds of stuff and didn't care that everyone was watching. Aunt Meg left me to go hang with her friends. I was standing in the corner, off by myself, when this guy comes up and offers me a drink. I told him that I didn't drink, and he said that it was just soda.

"I remember drinking it, then feeling like I was going to be sick. The next thing I knew, I was waking up in a bedroom with my clothes off. I was alone and scared. I got dressed and tried to find your aunt. When I finally found her, she was drunk and refused to listen to me or take me home. I walked home and found out three weeks later that I was pregnant. I told my mom and she kicked me out. I argued and tried to explain what happened, but it was no use. She said she would not have some tramp living in her house. I moved in with my Aunt Miranda and stayed there until Liza was three. Aunt Randi helped me out a lot. She would watch Liza so I could finish school and while I was working. I finally saved up enough money to live on our own. Granted it was not the best house, but it was a big enough apartment for us, and it was in a decent neighborhood.

"Two years later I met your dad. He was so sweet and caring. I think I fell in love with him the first time I saw him. We got married and had you. I didn't think life could be more perfect. But then, when you were about three, he started changing. He would make little snide remarks just to hurt my feelings. It just got worse and worse."

She paused long enough that Anna asked, "So, why did you stay with him?"

Melissa shrugged her shoulder. "Fear, I guess. I depended on him so much. After we got married, he didn't want me to work, so there was that. And, I don't know, maybe I thought that was how a marriage was supposed to be because that was how my dad was with my mom. George wasn't completely like my dad, though. He never did stuff in front of you girls. Maybe that's why I thought he was better than what he was. Looking back, I know that I should have left him, then maybe we would still have Liza." She started crying again.

"Mom," Anna said pulling her mom to her. "You can't blame yourself for something that someone else did. You didn't know what would happen. Nobody did."

"I know, I just wish that things could have been different."

"Me, too. Sad as it is, at least we know the truth now. I hate to say it, but I think I believe what Liza wrote. After hearing you say how he treated you, I don't know why I didn't see it."

"I didn't let you, or Liza. I didn't want you to have the kind of childhood that I did; always afraid to say the wrong thing, do the wrong thing. I wanted you to be happy and free-spirited. Maybe I tried a little too hard, because I didn't see what was going on in my own house."

"Nobody did, Mom. We can't change what happened, all we can do is learn from it. Thanks to you, and now Liza, I have learned what it means to sacrifice for love. I have also learned that there are better ways of ensuring happiness. I hate what happened, but I'm glad I know the truth now, even if I don't want to believe it."

"Me, too," Melissa whispered, wiping her tears.

"I have also learned that life will not always be easy. That we will have many battles we have to fight through, but as long as we have each other and God, everything will be just fine."

Coming Soon

Sadie Maxwell always dreamed that
one day her prince charming would
come riding in on his white horse
and sweep her off her feet.

What happens, though, when the
Sweet Prince isn't as
sweet?

Find out in:
A Secret No More